"Are you going to kiss me, Hunter?" Brenna asked.

"I cannot believe you said that," he replied with a groan.

"Why not?" She smiled. "You obviously were giving the matter some serious thought. I just wondered if you'd made up your mind yet."

He muttered, "For your information, I do not go around kissing women I don't know, Brenna."

"You know me. Well, sort of. You are sitting in my living room, and I've just had my hands all over the scratches on your chest. Oh, never mind. I just wanted you to know I'd enjoy it, but I wouldn't want you to compromise your principles."

"That's it," he said. "Enough!"

He grabbed her and pulled her into his lap, his mouth sweeping down onto hers in the same motion. Her eyes flew open in startled surprise, then drifted closed as she circled his neck with her arms. The kiss began as a rough, almost punishing embrace, but soon gentled to a sweet, sensuous caress that left both of them breathless . . .

WHAT ARE *LOVESWEPT* ROMANCES?

They are stories of true romance and touching emotion. We believe those two very important ingredients are constants in our highly sensual and very believable stories in the *LOVESWEPT* line. Our goal is to give you, the reader, stories of consistently high quality that may sometimes make you laugh, sometimes make you cry, but are always fresh and creative and contain many delightful surprises within their pages.

Most romance fans read an enormous number of books. Those they truly love, they keep. Others may be traded with friends and soon forgotten. We hope that each *LOVESWEPT* romance will be a treasure—a "keeper." We will always try to publish

LOVE STORIES YOU'LL NEVER FORGET
BY AUTHORS YOU'LL ALWAYS REMEMBER

The Editors

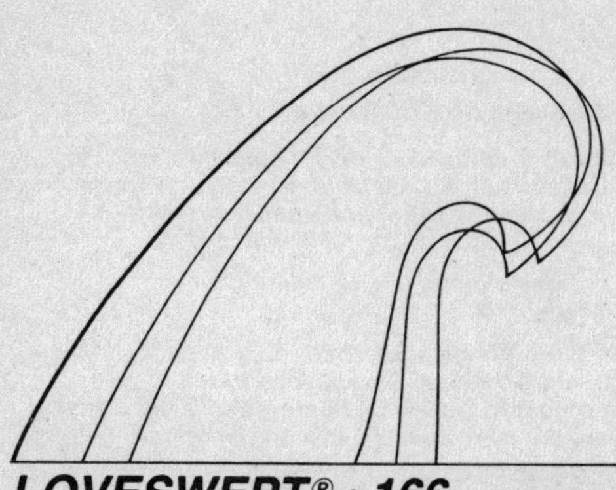

LOVESWEPT® • 166

Joan Elliott Pickart

Listen for the Drummer

BANTAM BOOKS
TORONTO • NEW YORK • LONDON • SYDNEY • AUCKLAND

LISTEN FOR THE DRUMMER
A Bantam Book / November 1986

LOVESWEPT® and the wave device are registered trademarks of Bantam Books, Inc. Registered in U.S. Patent and Trademark Office and elsewhere.

Cover art by George Tsui.

If you would be interested in receiving protective vinyl covers for your Loveswept books, please write to this address for information:

Loveswept
Bantam Books
P.O. Box 985
Hicksville, NY 11802

ISBN 0-553-21774-7

Published simultaneously in the United States and Canada

Bantam Books are published by Bantam Books, Inc. Its trademark, consisting of the words "Bantam Books" and the portrayal of a rooster, is Registered in U.S. Patent and Trademark Office and in other countries. Marca Registrada. Bantam Books, Inc., 666 Fifth Avenue, New York, New York 10103.

PRINTED IN THE UNITED STATES OF AMERICA

O 0 9 8 7 6 5 4 3 2 1

For my sister, Pat Elliott Hunt,
the nicest, bravest lobster I know

If a man does not keep pace
with his companions, perhaps it is
because he hears a different drummer.

Henry David Thoreau

One

He never saw it coming.

Hunter Emerson was strolling leisurely along the sidewalk deeply engrossed, as usual, in his own thoughts, when it hit him. Actually, it appeared to have flown out of nowhere.

A cat, a furry, screeching, howling cat landed with a thud against Hunter's chest and hung on for dear life, digging its claws into the material of Hunter's white shirt and his skin beneath.

Hunter stopped dead in his tracks and peered down in wide-eyed shock, his nose only inches from the open mouth of the animal, who was yowling at full volume. The claws dug deeper, and the message reached Hunter's brain.

"*Aaagh!*" he yelled, grabbing the beast. "Ouch! Oh! Dammit!"

The cat hung on.

Hunter bellowed and the cat continued to screech, then the duet was joined by the barking of a dog. In the next instant, Hunter was hit full force on the thighs and was down, flat on his back on the sidewalk. The cat beat a hasty retreat, and was replaced by a large white dog, who wiggled with delight and slathered a wet kiss over Hunter's face.

"Dammit to hell!" Hunter yelled.

A female voice joined the chorus. "Cookie, get off that man!" the voice said. "That is rude, very rude. Move right now, do you hear me, you naughty boy?"

Cookie gave Hunter one more slobbery kiss, then retreated, sitting down on the sidewalk and thumping his tail excitedly.

Hunter groaned, his arms limp on the pavement, and closed his eyes.

Brenna MacPhee gasped in horror as she stared at the prone man, then dropped to her knees beside him, patting him lightly on the cheek.

"Hello?" she said. "You're not dead, are you? Oh, please, mister, tell me you're not dead. I just couldn't handle it!" She bent closer, then closer yet, as she scrutinized his face. "Hello?" she said hopefully.

Hunter opened one blue eye and stared into one brown eye.

"Oh, thank heavens, you're alive!" Brenna said, moving back slightly.

Hunter opened his other eye and moaned. "What in the hell happened?" he said, starting to sit up.

"Don't move," Brenna said, splaying her hands on his chest. "You might be broken. You went down awfully hard. I really am so sorry about this. Oh! Oh! There's blood on your shirt!"

"What do you expect? I've been attacked by a mountain lion and a horse!" Hunter said, none too quietly. He brushed Brenna's hand away and staggered to his feet. "I can't believe this!"

"Actually," Brenna said, "it was a cat and a dog, but I can understand why you're upset. How do you feel?"

"Like committing murder! I'm bleeding to death, every bone in my body hurts, I probably have . . ." He gingerly probed the back of his head. "Yes, I do! There's a lump on my head!"

Brenna chewed on her bottom lip as she stared up at the tall, angry man. He was, she decided, extremely handsome. Mad as hell, but handsome. His eyes were the most remarkable shade of blue, his mouth beautifully shaped. His hair, which was presently tousled, appeared thick and was the color of sable with auburn highlights. He had wide shoulders, muscular legs clad in dark slacks, which were spotted with white dog fur . . . Nice. Just really, really nice. And the next words out of his mouth were probably going to be that he planned to sue the pants off her!

"Hi!" she said brightly. "I'm Brenna MacPhee. I think we should go to my place and let me tend to those scratches. Oh, and I'll put an ice cube on your head. I'll fix you up as good as new."

"Lady," Hunter growled, "do I look like I have a death wish? I wouldn't go anywhere with you! You're a menace!"

"I am not! That cat wasn't mine. I'm trying to be a good samaritan here." And hopefully not get sued, she added silently.

"Well, that dog is obviously yours, and he was chasing the cat."

"Cookie isn't mine. Well, for now he is, but . . . Please let me see to your injuries. My place is right down the block. Come on," she said, grabbing Hunter's arm.

"Oh, my aching body," he said, allowing himself to be led down the sidewalk. Cookie joined them, tail still wagging, his tongue hanging out of the side of his mouth.

What a strong arm, Brenna mused, as she hauled her cargo along. "What's your name?" she asked.

"Hunter Emerson," he said, checking the condition of his head again. "It's getting bigger. The lump is getting bigger!"

"I have lots of ice," Brenna said, patting his hand. "Don't worry about a thing."

"Hell!"

"I wish you wouldn't swear in front of Cookie. He's very sensitive."

The next expletive Hunter uttered was a beaut, and Brenna decided to keep silent on the subject of Cookie's delicate ears.

"Here we are," she said, stopping in front of a small house. "Just up the walk and in the door, then we'll get you taken care of."

"I think it would be better if I went on home."

"Nonsense," she said, and led him into the house.

Hunter mentally threw up his hands, and was soon standing in a living room that had been decorated to resemble the lobby of an old-fashioned hotel. There was a registration counter with numbered mail slots behind it, a grouping of overstuffed furniture, and a player piano. A huge Boston fern hung in the front window, and a variety of other plants were scattered throughout the room.

"You rent rooms?" Hunter asked, glancing around.

"Yes. My apartment is upstairs."

She walked across the hardwood floor to the staircase against the far wall. Cookie bounded up the stairs first, then Brenna, with Hunter a slow third. From his vantage point, he had a clear view of Brenna's bottom, which was outlined to perfection in faded jeans. He'd been so startled by the chain of events that had transpired, he hadn't really taken a good look at Brenna MacPhee. As she reached the top of the stairs and turned to smile down at him, he made up for lost time.

Cute, he thought. She was adorably cute. She had a riot of blond curls that tumbled to her shoulders, large brown eyes, and small features. She herself wasn't very big, maybe five four, and at six feet he would seem to tower over her. Her breasts were small and firm beneath her red T-shirt. There was a pixielike quality about her, and her smile lit up her whole face. She also owned a dog that had nearly killed him!

"Look, Miss MacPhee," Hunter said as he joined her at the top of the stairs, "I'll just go on home. It is miss, isn't it?"

"Yes, but call me Brenna. After all, Cookie splattered you all over the pavement, so it's a little late to stand on formality. Of course, the cat is equally responsible. Are your eyes really that blue? Or are those colored contact lenses?"

"I beg your pardon?"

"Your eyes. They really are a fantastic shade of blue. I just wondered if they were yours. Well, you know what I mean."

"They're mine," he said, frowning slightly. "Do

you always jump from one subject to the next so quickly? Never mind. It probably just seems like you do because my head hurts."

"Oh, good heavens, your head!" Brenna said, spinning around and marching down the hall. "And your chest! You're a member of the walking wounded, and I'm standing around chatting about your bedroom eyes."

"Bedroom eyes?" Hunter muttered, following her down the hall.

"Cookie, lie down," Brenna said when they entered her living room. "Mr. Emerson, please sit there on the sofa while I gather my first-aid supplies."

"It's Hunter," he said absently as she left. His gaze swept over the room. "Strange," he said under his breath.

Again, plants were in abundance, but there was no real motif to the room. The sofa was a faded pattern of black with large pink flowers, and even from where he stood it appeared lumpy. A weather-beaten coffee table sat in front of it and an orange chair beside it. Against the far wall was a bookcase packed to overflowing, a small stereo, and a stack of magazines on the floor. A rolltop desk was barely visible beneath its burden of papers and sundry other items. The only thing in the room with a semblance of order was a glass shelf above the desk, where a collection of four small unicorns sat.

Hunter wandered across the room and peered at the figurines. The tiniest unicorn was pewter, and no more than an inch high. One was solid white, another clear crystal, and the fourth, and largest, at perhaps three inches, was carved out of teakwood.

"Here we go," Brenna said cheerfully, coming back into the room carrying a tray. "Please sit down, Mr. Emerson."

"Hunter," he said, turning to face her.

"All right, Hunter. We have to get organized. Unbutton your shirt so I can clean the scratches, and you hold this ice pack on your head. Have you had a tetanus shot lately?"

"Yes, but . . . Maybe I should go see my own doctor."

"Oh, don't worry. I earned my First Aid Badge when I was in Girl Scouts."

"Wonderful," he muttered. He sat down on the sofa, deciding it was lumpier than it looked, and pulled his shirt free of his pants. He unbuttoned it and spread it open, then glanced up at Brenna. Her gaze was riveted on his bare chest.

"You have the most beautiful chest I've ever seen," she said wistfully.

"What?" he croaked.

"You do!" she said, sitting down on the coffee table. "So tanned, nicely muscled, yummy soft curls. But then, I'm sure women tell you that all the time. Here, put this ice pack on the back of your head. Are you in the military?"

"Huh?" Hunter said, pressing the ice pack to his head.

"You wear your hair quite short. I thought you might be in the service."

"No, I'm not," he snapped. "I happen to like my hair like this. At least it doesn't look like I stuck my finger in an electric socket!"

She laughed. "This is my new perm," she said, fluffing her curls with her hand. "I adore it. I was hoping it would make me look older, but no such luck. I still like it, though."

"How old *are* you?" he asked. Lord, she had an enchanting laugh, he thought. But trying to keep track of what she was saying was next to impossible! He had a beautiful chest? He'd never had any complaints about his body, but no one had ever commented quite like *that* before.

"I'm twenty-four," she said. "And, yes, I know, I look younger. Okay, grit your teeth because this antiseptic might sting. How old are you?"

"Twenty-nine—ow!" he said, as she pressed a cotton ball to one of the scratches.

"Sorry. I'll try to hurry. They don't look too bad, considering the way that cat was attached to you."

"Due to the fact that it was being chased by your dog," Hunter said gruffly. "I would think you'd keep him on a leash when you take him out."

"Oh, we weren't going for a walk. Cookie knows how to turn doorknobs with his teeth."

"You're kidding."

"Nope. His owners warned me about it, but I forgot for a moment and left the door unlocked. He can't do locks. Anyway, he turned the knob and *poof!* he was gone. Good thing I caught up with him. It would never do for me to lose one of my guests."

"Here we go again," Hunter said, sighing. "Brenna, what are you talking about? You said you rented out rooms."

"I do! To animals. This is the Pet Palace, a place for people to leave their pets when they go on vacation. Did you notice the lobby? I fixed it up like an old-fashioned hotel. Cute, huh? Do you know that people actually send postcards to their pets?"

"And I suppose you read them to them."

"Oh, well, sure. This last scratch is the worst. You can yell if you want to."

She leaned closer to press the cotton ball to his chest, and he caught the lemony fresh aroma of her hair. He had the irrational urge to sink his fingers into the honey-colored curls to see if they were as silky as they looked. He had never met anyone like Brenna MacPhee before. She was a very unusual young woman, and definitely not his type. She was scatterbrained, totally unorganized by the looks of her living room, and hardly made sense half the time. She read postcards to animals? Lord. And what the hell was the matter with the length of his hair?

"Done," Brenna said, lifting her head to look at him. "And, Hunter? I really am very sorry about what happened."

Hunter started to speak, but no words came as he looked directly into Brenna's large brown eyes. The thoughts that skittered through his mind disturbed him, but still he didn't tear his gaze from hers. He wanted to kiss this woman, he realized, hold her close to him, feel her slight form pressed to his body.

Hunter Emerson was not one to fantasize. He lived in the real world of logic, facts and figures, proof from gathered data. He also dealt with computers, which reproduced on a green screen exactly what they had been programmed to do. There was no logical reason, he told himself, why he should have such a burning desire to haul Brenna MacPhee into his arms and cover her lips with his. Granted, she was attractive, but that certainly wasn't enough to evoke such uncharacteristic urges within himself. His reaction to Brenna didn't make sense and, therefore, he didn't like it!

"Are you going to kiss me, Hunter?" Brenna asked.

"Oh, Lord!" he said, rolling his eyes heavenward. "I can't believe you said that."

"Why not?" she asked, shrugging. "You obviously are giving serious thought to the subject. I just wondered if you were going to do it. I wouldn't mind, if that's what's concerning you."

"I've frozen my brain," he said, scowling as he tossed the ice pack onto the coffee table. "Delayed shock. Yes, I'm suffering from delayed shock from a trauma to my body. Brenna, I do not go around kissing women I don't even know!"

"You know me. Well, sort of. You're sitting in my living room, and I've had my hands all over your beautiful chest. Well, never mind. I just thought sharing a kiss with you would be very enjoyable, but I wouldn't want you to compromise your principles."

"That's it," he said. "I've had it!"

He grabbed her by the upper arms and lifted her onto his lap, his mouth sweeping down onto hers in the same motion. Her eyes flew open in startled surprise, then drifted closed as she circled his neck with her arms.

The kiss began as a rough, almost punishing embrace, then gentled to sweet, soft, and sensuous. Hunter drank of Brenna's sweetness, inhaled her fresh feminine aroma, and desire rocketed through his body. He ran his tongue over her lower lip, seeking entry to the darkness of her mouth. She opened to him, and he explored every secret crevice, then found her tongue and dueled seductively with it. His hands roamed over her back, then one slid down to her firm breast, on to the gentle curve of her waist, and along her leg. His hold on her tightened as the kiss deepened, their breathing becoming labored in the quiet room.

Brenna savored the taste and feel of Hunter Emerson. Her body hummed with pure sensuality like never before. Where he was tight and hard, she was soft, and they fit together like pieces of a jigsaw puzzle. His large hands ignited heated passion as they skimmed over her. Her breasts were taut, aching, wanting the sweet magic of his mouth. The rhythmic thrusting of his tongue against hers was matched by a pulsing cadence deep within her.

Hunter tore his mouth away and drew a ragged breath, his chest heaving. With trembling hands he lifted her from his lap and set her next to him, then ran his hand down his face.

"I'm sorry," he said, his voice strained. "I really didn't mean to do that."

"Did you hate it?" Brenna asked, her own voice unsteady.

"Are you crazy?" he snapped, turning to look at her, his blue eyes still smoky with desire. "That was one helluva kiss we just shared, lady!"

"Oh," she said, smiling at him. "I'm glad you enjoyed it, because I certainly did. I must say, Hunter, you're a superb kisser. You really are. Excellent, in fact. Would you care for a glass of lemonade?"

"Hold it just a damn minute," he said, pushing himself to his feet and glaring down at her. "What are you doing? Conducting a kissing survey in Portland, Oregon?"

She laughed. "Don't be silly."

"Do you kiss all your men the way you did me?"

"Lips on lips? That's usually how it's done, Hunter."

"That's not what I mean!"

"What are you yelling about?"

"I have no idea," he said, shaking his head slightly. "I really don't. I think I'll go home, take two aspirin, and lie down. This past hour has not come remotely close to making sense. And there is absolutely, positively no logical explanation for my behavior. I wonder if I have a concussion?"

Brenna frowned as she got to her feet. "Do you always have to have a logical explanation for everything you do?" she asked.

"Of course," he said as he buttoned his shirt. "I own a consulting firm that deals in cost analysis. The information is gathered and fed into computers using specialized programs. Everything, every detail, is analyzed, calculated, projected, so that the end product is error-free, perfect. There's no room in my life to go off on a whim."

She planted her hands on her hips. "Kissing me was a whim?"

"I'm not sure what that was," he said, staring into space. "I can't remember when I've ever done anything so impulsive."

"Impulsive or not, I thought it was terrific," Brenna said cheerfully, winding a blond curl around her finger.

"Yeah, I know," he said, jamming his shirt into his pants. "You keep score cards or something.

Will you look at the dog hair on my slacks? Sheesh, I'm a total wreck."

"Want me to brush it off?" Brenna asked, reaching out her hand.

"No!" he said, taking a step backward. "I mean, no, thank you. I'll take care of it. Well, it was quite an experience meeting you, Brenna. I hope you remember to keep the doors locked during the remainder of Cookie's stay at your hotel."

"Oh, I certainly will. And I apologize again for what happened. Oh, not for sharing the kiss, because that was great. I meant the bump on your head and the cat scratches."

"Well, it really wasn't your fault, I guess. I appreciate the first aid. You must have been a fairly good Girl Scout."

"I flunked making campfires," she said, and smiled.

Dammit! he thought. Why did she have to look at him like that? He wanted to kiss her again, he really did! What was it with her, this Brenna MacPhee? He had to get out of here. Now!

"Gotta go," he said briskly, tearing his gaze from hers. He strode to the door. "Good-bye, Brenna."

"Bye," she said softly.

Hunter hesitated a moment, then left the apartment, his footsteps echoing as he bounded down the stairs.

Brenna sighed and sank onto the sofa, pressing her fingertips to her lips. Hunter Emerson, she mused. Oh, he was beautiful. Even his voice, so rich and deep, had caused her pulse to skitter. And when he'd kissed her, her bones had seemed to dissolve as she'd clung to him for support. But he hadn't smiled, not once. He was just so serious, so . . . What had he said? He had a logical explanation for everything he did. Ugh. How boring. He was, apparently, some kind of analytical genius, who dealt in numbers and computers. Anything to do with math boggled her mind, and computers made her nervous. She always had the impression they were smarter than she was. Well, one thing was for darn sure. Hunter was a wingding of a kisser!

She had felt something new, something different when Hunter had kissed her. She was not a blushing innocent at the ripe old age of twenty-four, but never before had she been filled with such startling and wondrous sensations as she had while being kissed by Hunter Emerson.

Cookie woke from his nap, yawned and stretched, then padded over to Brenna and plopped his head in her lap.

"Wasn't Hunter something, Cookie?" she said. "The trouble with this whole thing is, I'll never see him again. And that, my furry friend, is a rotten shame." She pulled on one of her curls, felt it bounce back into place, reaffirmed in her mind that the perm was outstanding, then patted Cookie on the head. "Come on," she said. "It's time to check on the other guests."

When Hunter emerged from Brenna's he glanced around in confusion. He'd done it again, he realized. He was lost. On more occasions than he cared to remember, he'd left his office for a walk to sort through a particularly difficult cost-analysis problem, and paid no attention to where he was going. How someone as organized as he was could continually do that, he didn't know, but here he was again, lost.

He was on a tree-lined street, that much he knew. The old houses were a variety of styles and sizes, and the majority seemed to be businesses. He vaguely remembered a zoning ordinance that was passed in Portland a few years ago involving several square blocks of a residential area. The home owners were given the right to conduct businesses within their dwellings if they chose to do so.

Yep, that was where he was, all right. Nearly two miles from his office. His head ached, his clothes were a disaster, and he had a real trek ahead of him. Wonderful, he thought, starting off down the sidewalk.

This time he paid attention to where he was going and saw that this entire block housed various enterprises. He passed a bakery, several specialty boutiques, and an Italian restaurant. He could go inside someplace and call for a taxi, he supposed, but maybe the walk would do him good. And maybe the walk would erase the last lingering thoughts of Brenna MacPhee from his mind.

Brenna MacPhee. He rolled the sound through his mind, adding a Scottish burr to the obviously Scottish name. She was, without a doubt, the most exhausting woman he had ever met. The mere effort of keeping up with her disjointed conversations was enough to tax a man's mental capabilities. She said whatever popped into her head, from the subject of the length of his hair, to the glorious condition of his chest, to a rating of his kissing expertise.

And that was another thing. Why in the hell had he kissed her? He wasn't a hustler, a grabber. He respected women, dated them when he found the time, slept with a few like any healthy, red-blooded male. But he sure didn't kiss the living daylights out of a woman he'd known for less than an hour. He didn't, that is, until Brenna MacPhee.

Well, he'd suffered a trauma, he rationalized. It wasn't every day that a man was attacked by a screaming cat, flattened by an overzealous dog, then thrown off kilter by a pixie of a woman with a hairdo like Shirley Temple. He was fine now, back to normal. Clean clothes, two aspirin, and all would be well. He just wished he could erase from his memory the taste, the aroma, the feel of Brenna MacPhee. He did not, of course, compare kisses like some kind of adolescent. But if he did, just supposing that he did, Brenna's kiss would go right off the Richter scale. There was a very passionate woman in that tiny bundle of energy.

"Forget it," he muttered, quickening his step. "Just forget the whole damn thing. She really reads postcards to those animals? Lord."

In the kitchen of the Pet Palace, Brenna prepared dinner for the three cats in residence, then carried the cuisine to the second bedroom upstairs. The cages were open, and the cats were engaged in rough-and-tumble play on the floor. Cookie was given a firm directive to remain in the hall.

The dogs were housed in the downstairs bedroom off the kitchen, and her current guests were a Saint Bernard, a miniature poodle, and the ever-famous nondescript Cookie. In the laundry room was a pair of caged yellow canaries.

After all the animals had been fed and the dogs

had been let out in their respective runways in the backyard, Brenna prepared her own meal of salad, a hamburger, and a huge bowl of chocolate-chip ice cream. She ate the ice cream along with the hamburger and salad, having decided long ago that it made no sense to wait to consume the really good part of dinner. But tonight the food went untasted. One thought, one image, filled her mind. Hunter Emerson.

Beautiful, beautiful Hunter, she mused, absently stirring her ice cream into a soupy mess. She adored his hair, even though it was cut too short. It was the shade of sable, or chestnuts, several tones darker than an Irish setter's. Gorgeous. *He* was gorgeous, head to toe. She really wanted to see him again. Oh, and, of course, share another one of his mind-boggling kisses. Or maybe two kisses. Or a dozen. No doubt about it, the guy had gotten to her.

Brenna sighed, then stared down in amazement at her ice cream. With a shrug she ate it anyway, still thinking of Hunter.

Hunter Emerson was not a happy man.

By the time he'd hiked back to his office, everyone had left for the day. Contrary to his usual mode of organized behavior, he had gone for his walk without his keys, and had to find the security officer to let him in. No, he had not been mugged, he had told the man, but attacked by a mountain lion. The security officer had said Hunter was a real card.

Once in his office, Hunter washed and changed into a clean pair of dark slacks and white shirt. He kept some clothes in his office since it wasn't unusual for him to spend the night on the sofa here when he was involved in a complicated project.

He also kept food in a small refrigerator, and he made a sandwich, poured himself a glass of milk, then settled onto the leather chair in front of his computer. And through it all, he thought of Brenna. He loaded a disk into the machine, then swore when he heard a beep and the screen announced a syntax error. And still he thought of Brenna.

Why he couldn't dismiss her from his mind, he didn't know. What he was going to do about it, he didn't know either. She was driving him nuts! The situation called for what he did best—logical, rational reasoning.

Brenna MacPhee did not fall into any category of women he knew. She was different. Brother, was she ever! Slightly weird was an apt description. She didn't fit into a mold, and so she had a touch of mystique. That made sense. All he had to do was see her again, just once, figure out what made her tick, then that would be that. Hunter liked his life in order with no loose ends. The fact that Brenna was taking up his brain space was disturbing and not acceptable.

He strode to his desk and flipped through the telephone book until he found the listing for the Pet Palace. He punched out the numbers, and drummed his fingers impatiently on the desk as the phone rang, and rang, and rang.

"Pet Palace," a cheerful voice finally answered.

"Brenna?"

"Yes."

"This is Hunter Emerson."

"Hello, Hunter," she said. "How's your head?"

"Fine, fine. Did I interrupt a party there?"

"What? Oh, no. Some friends of mine dropped by. A few of them brought their instruments and we're having a jam session."

Hunter could hear a clarinet wailing in the background, and shook his head. "I see. Brenna, would you have dinner with me tomorrow night?"

"Well, yes, that sounds lovely."

"Good. Seven o'clock. Good-bye."

"Bye," she said to the dial tone, then laughed. "If you weren't Scottish, I'd say you had the luck of the Irish, Brenna MacPhee."

Two

Typical of Portland weather, it rained most of the next day. There was a crispness to the mid-September air, signaling the arrival of autumn that would bring with it the spectacle of color when the leaves began to change on the trees.

Brenna spent the majority of the day cleaning the animals' enclosures, then dashed outside between rain showers to shovel and rake the dog runs. She was drenched more than once, and was delighted with the performance of her permanent. Her riot of honey-colored curls bounced back into place when toweled dry.

Like a mother with small children, Brenna kept a list of reliable baby-sitters who would come to the Pet Palace to care for her charges when she decided to go out for the evening. All were students at the University of Portland, and had been carefully interviewed to assure their love for animals.

Brenna's first choice was always Cindy Cole, a

sophomore majoring in home economics. Cindy was a short, plump, vivacious redhead, whose very round figure testified to the fact that she enjoyed sampling the various dishes she was learning to prepare in her classes.

Brenna called Cindy, who said she was available for that night. She was delighted to learn that Cookie was presently a guest, as the furry white dog was everyone's favorite. And, yes, Cindy said, she'd keep the doors securely locked so there would be no chance of Cookie escaping from the Palace.

Brenna fed the animals their dinners, then at six o'clock stepped into the shower. She blow-dried her hair, creating a golden halo of curls around her face. A few quick strokes of mascara and a rose lip gloss were the full extent of her makeup. A light, floral-scented cologne was whiffed over her slender throat, then Brenna turned to her closet.

The pale pink gauze dress seemed to float about her as she tied the matching sash around her small waist. The neckline scooped to the edge of her lightly tanned shoulders, and the tiered skirt fell almost to her ankles. She slipped her feet into simple thin-strapped heels and buckled them into place. Stepping back to survey her reflection in the full-length mirror, she nodded in approval.

She looked very nice, she decided, and she was definitely enthusiastic about the evening ahead. Hunter had snuck into her thoughts constantly during the day, and she freely admitted she was eager to see him. It was due in part, she knew, to the lingering memories of his sensuous kiss, but it was more than that. An unknown something had kept him close to the front of her mind. Why she was so intrigued by a man who had yet to even smile at her, she didn't know.

A buzzer sounded and she walked to the box on the wall next to the living-room door.

"Yes?" she said, after pressing a button.

"Hi, Brenna. It's Cindy."

"Come on up." She pushed a lever that released the lock on the front door, then heard Cindy's footsteps on the stairs. "Hi," she said, opening the door. "All set to baby-sit my babies?"

"Sure," Cindy said, coming into the room. "Hello, Cookie my love. It's so good to see you." Cookie wiggled in delight. "Oh, Brenna, you look gorgeous. Who's the lucky hunk who has the honor of your company tonight?"

"His name is Hunter Emerson, and he's beautiful."

"Really? Where did you find him?"

"Cookie smashed him flat, right onto the sidewalk. Being the humanitarian that I am, I brought him up here to tend to his wounds. He was in a rather lousy mood, but he was still beautiful."

"Well," Cindy said, flopping onto the lumpy sofa, "he couldn't have been too put off. You do have a date with him."

"Which totally surprised me. I never thought I'd see him again. Is it cold out?"

"Nippy. A shawl will do. That magenta one with the fringe would look super with that dress."

"All I have to do is find it," Brenna said, heading back into the bedroom. "If I were a shawl, where would I hide?"

The buzzer sounded again. "Cindy," Brenna called, "will you please answer that? If it's Hunter, unlatch the door."

"Okay," Cindy said. "This is the upstairs maid," she said into the intercom. "Please state your business with Her Highness."

Hunter jerked in surprise at the sound of an unfamiliar voice speaking to him from a small box on the porch. A sign posted on the front door stated that if the door was locked, please press the buzzer. He had done that, but the voice had definitely caught him off guard. He peered at the box, then tentatively pushed a button.

"Hunter Emerson to see Brenna MacPhee," he said, feeling utterly foolish.

"Enter, Noble Knight," the voice said, then the latch popped on the door and Hunter jumped again.

He stepped into the downstairs living room and looked around for the owner of the voice. A smiling, red-haired girl was standing on the stairs.

"Hi," she said. "I'm Cindy Cole. Come on up. Brenna is just about ready. Oh, be careful where you step. Three guinea pigs checked in today, and they're having their nightly exercise. They're cute little buggers. So much better than the boa constrictor. I really hated it when that snake was here."

"Lord," Hunter muttered, checking the floor before he strode to the stairs. He followed Cindy to Brenna's living room, then stopped in the doorway when Cookie bounded toward him. "Go away, dog," he said.

"Cookie, sit," Brenna commanded from the bedroom doorway. "For heaven's sake, he did! He's never obeyed that command before. Hello, Hunter," she added, smiling at him.

"Hello," he said, "you look . . . very lovely,

Brenna." What was she wearing? he wondered. It looked like a pink tablecloth. The shawl was an absurd shade, but somehow it was right on her. A happy, crazy color, not remotely close to gaudy. She was very attractive, in an offbeat sort of way.

"I assume you met Cindy," Brenna said, picking up her purse. "She's my baby-sitter tonight."

"Your what?" he asked.

"I never leave my guests alone for an evening. I feel it would be irresponsible on my part. Cindy, you know where their snacks are for later, and help yourself to whatever you'd like."

"Don't worry about a thing," Cindy said. "We'll all be fine. Oh, and don't feel you have to hurry home. I can always sleep right here on the sofa if I get tired. It's more comfortable than my bed at the dorm, anyway."

"You're kidding," Hunter said.

"Pardon me?" Cindy said.

"Nothing. It was nice meeting you, Cindy. Ready, Brenna?"

"Brenna," Cindy said, "may I see you in the bedroom for a teeny little minute?"

"Of course," Brenna said. "I'll be right back, Hunter." He nodded.

In the bedroom, Brenna looked at Cindy questioningly as the younger woman closed the door.

"Oh, Brenna," Cindy said in a loud whisper, "Hunter is unbelievable! He's so tall, so good-looking, so tanned, so—so everything! He's dressed like he's going to a funeral, but other than that he's perfect! If you let Hunter Emerson get away, I'll absolutely die!"

"I can't lock him in one of the animal enclosures," Brenna said, laughing. "But he really is beautiful, isn't he?"

"Oh, yes! Except for the clothes. Black suit and tie, white shirt. He looks like an undertaker."

"That's okay," Brenna said. "My pink on pink is bright enough for both of us. I—oh, good Lord, we left him alone with Cookie!"

Brenna yanked open the door and hurried back into the living room. She stopped so abruptly that Cindy, right on her heels, bumped into her, nearly knocking her over.

Hunter was pointing a long finger at Cookie, who was wiggling around on the floor, wagging his tail, but making no attempt to leap at Hunter.

"Pretty good, huh?" Hunter said. "I told him to stay, and he is. His tail may fall off from overuse, but he's staying put."

And then there it was, the smile.

The stern features of Hunter's tanned face gentled. Tiny lines crinkled at the corners of his eyes, and his white teeth flashed as his beautiful mouth curved up. His blue eyes sparkled like clear, bright sapphires.

Brenna was hardly aware that Cindy had dropped to her knees beside Cookie and was praising the dog for his excellent behavior. Brenna was riveted in place, unable to tear her gaze from Hunter's face as her heart beat wildly. Hunter was looking directly at her, and neither moved, nor hardly seemed to breathe.

Then Hunter's smile slowly faded and was replaced by a frown that drew his brows together. He cleared his throat, snapping the eerie tension that had settled over them. Brenna blinked as if coming out of a trance.

"Shall we go?" Hunter said gruffly.

"Yes," Brenna said, her voice hushed. "Good-bye, Cindy."

"Bye, guys," Cindy said, bouncing to her feet. "Have fun, and don't even look at a clock. Cookie and I will hold down the fort with no problems."

As Hunter followed Brenna down the stairs, he caught the tantalizing aroma of her cologne. He studied her soft curls, and felt the irrational urge to sink his hands into the silken cascade. Dammit, what was it about her? he silently fumed. When their eyes had met across the room he couldn't have moved if someone had put a gun to his head. She was dressed like a gypsy. Maybe she was a gypsy and had cast a spell over him— That was crazy!

Outside, he led Brenna to his car and helped her in. After sliding behind the wheel he glanced over at her, and she smiled at him. He snapped his head back, turned the key in the ignition, and pulled away from the curb.

"I just realized," Brenna said, "that I didn't ask if you were married. I always do that before I accept a date with a man, but I forgot."

"I'm not married."

"I probably knew that subconsciously. After all, you'd have gone home to your wife yesterday to have your wounds tended to. Are you from Portland?"

"Yes. My parents live here, but my two sisters have moved away. They're both married and have children, and one lives in Los Angeles, the other in Dallas."

"Are your parents eager for you to have a son to carry on the Emerson name?"

"Yes, they are," he said, looking at her in surprise. "They bug me about it all the time."

"Are you going to? Have children?"

"I don't know," he said, lifting one shoulder in a shrug. "I've been concentrating on getting my company, Hunter Emerson Consulting Corporation, off the ground. I don't have enough hours in the day as it is."

"I'm going to have a baby," Brenna said.

"What?" he croaked.

"I'm not sure when, but someday. It'll be glorious, creating a child with the man I love, then watching my body change, grow big with that new life. Think about it, Hunter. Two mere humans, but their union has resulted in a miracle. A man and a woman join together in—"

"Brenna!" Hunter said loudly as heat shot across the lower regions of his body.

"Yes?"

"I thought we'd eat at Captain's Corner."

"Lovely."

He wasn't going to survive this, he thought. He never knew what she was going to say! Hadn't she ever heard of idle chitchat? Not Brenna. She went rattling on about making love and getting pregnant, for Pete's sake!

How would she look with a child suckling at her breast? he wondered. Serene, glowing? Yes, she'd have an aura of beauty and— Dammit! Why couldn't she discuss the state of the economy?

He shook his head slightly as he merged with the traffic on the Broadway Bridge over the Willamette River.

"Do *you* have family?" he asked, hoping to the heavens it was a safe question to ask her.

"Just my father. The MacPhee is in the Canadian wilderness at the moment, somewhere along the western coast. I'm not exactly sure why. He doesn't always tell me why he's going where he's going. Actually, I'm not certain he knows himself why he's in a particular spot."

Hunter frowned. "How long have you been on your own?"

"Since I was eighteen. Oh, the MacPhee visits when he can. He isn't content to stay in one spot for long, though. I've lived in so many states, I've lost track. But now I have a real home at the Pet Palace, and I adore it. I don't think I'll ever budge again. Portland is so beautiful, and I've made such marvelous friends here. I'm very impressed with the way you got Cookie to obey you, Hunter. He has a tendency to be rather scatterbrained."

"Back up here," Hunter said. "Your father, 'the MacPhee' as you call him, left you when you were only eighteen? Where's your mother?"

"I never knew her. The MacPhee said she was more of a dreamer than even he was, and went off with the first man who promised her a pot of gold. But, yes, he did go when I graduated from high school. It was time for me to look after myself. I was terribly frightened at first, but I did all right. From the way you're frowning, I assume you don't approve, but I understand the MacPhee. He loves me, Hunter. I've never doubted that. He just marches to the tune of a different drummer."

"I see," Hunter said, but he really didn't. This MacPhee added up to a selfish crumb, he thought. How could a father walk away from a child fresh out of high school? A child he'd dragged around the country all of her life like so much extra baggage. Damn, what a lousy hand Brenna had been dealt. And she was thrilled to live with a bunch of animals in an old house with a lumpy sofa?

"We all have to do that," Brenna said, bringing Hunter from his reverie. "Listen for the drummer, know who we are, what we need to make us happy. But then, you already know that."

"I do?" he asked, glancing over at her. She wasn't making much sense. She talked as though some guy in a band uniform marched up and told everyone where they belonged. "What drummer?"

"The one inside you, your inner voice, your true self. Surely you heard the tune or you wouldn't have worked so hard toward your dream of owning your consulting company. That was your dream, wasn't it?"

"Well, yeah."

"See? Did your parents understand?"

"Not really. My father assumed I'd become a lawyer and join his firm. I think he's still waiting for me to come to my senses, get my law degree, marry, produce the Emerson heir. He's never even visited my office to see what I've done. My mother has, but my father refuses. Things are pretty strained when I go to the house." Dammit, Hunter thought, why was he telling her all this? He didn't bare his soul to anyone, let alone a woman he barely knew!

Taking Brenna to dinner was a mistake, he decided. He should have attributed the fact that he couldn't get her off his mind to his whack on the head. He should have forgotten her *and* the kiss they'd shared, that sweet, wonderful kiss he hadn't wanted to end. He'd thought by seeing her again, he'd figure out what made her tick. Ha! The ticking of a clock was a steady, back-and-forth motion.

Brenna didn't tick, she zoomed. She zipped around from one topic to the next, sitting still only long enough to see if her damn drummer wanted to rap out a message or something.

"You certainly frown a lot, Hunter," Brenna said, interrupting his thoughts again. "You're going to get premature wrinkles. You have such a wonderful smile. You should use it more often."

Oh, terrific, he thought. Now he had a wonderful smile to go with his fantastic eyes and beautiful chest. The thing was, he knew Brenna wasn't being coy or flirtatious when she said those things. She was merely expressing her opinion, and saw no reason why she shouldn't. How was a guy supposed to respond to statements like that? She was so unsettling. And, dammit, he still couldn't erase the memory of taking her into his arms and kissing her. Enough was enough. He'd buy her dinner, then take her straight home. He was getting Brenna MacPhee out of his life.

"Hunter," Brenna said, "why did you invite me out tonight?"

"What?"

"Well, if you have a logical reason for everything you do, then there must be a logical reason why we're going to dinner. I just wondered what it was."

"How about, because we both had to eat?" he said, smiling at her.

"Oh," she said, nodding. That smile! she thought. What it did to her was sinful!

"You believe that explanation?" he asked.

"No, of course not, but I'm not going to get pushy about it. I was just curious, because I've never met anyone who thinks like you do, and I'm trying to understand you better."

"*That* is why we're here," he said, turning onto the drive that led to the restaurant. "I've never met anyone like you before, either, and I can't figure you out."

"Really? Goodness, I'm the most ordinary person I know."

Hunter opened his mouth, then shut it when he realized he didn't know what to say. He handed the car keys to the parking valet, then lightly cupped Brenna's elbow as he escorted her into the restaurant. It had been designed for what was advertised as intimate dining, and they were led to a cozy candle-lit table. Hunter selected a fine wine for them, then they ordered from the extensive menu.

The flickering candlelight sent dancing shadows over Hunter's handsome face, and Brenna stared at him, fascinated by the play of light. Their salads were served, and Hunter buttered a roll. Her gaze followed the bread to his mouth, watched his white teeth take a bite, his jaw move as he chewed.

There was nothing sexy, she told herself, about a man chomping on a roll. But then again, Hunter Emerson probably looked sexy brushing his teeth! He must have tons of women swarming after him, she thought. Worldly, sophisticated women, no doubt, not a working girl like herself. Did he sleep with those women? Probably. There was no reason why not. He was gorgeous. With that face and body, who would notice that he didn't smile very often? What would it be like, she wondered wistfully, to be made love to by Hunter Emerson? To have all that virility, that masculinity, directed at her?

"Don't you like salad?" Hunter asked.

"What? Oh, sure I do," she said, and immediately took a bite. "So," she said, "tell me everything I ever wanted to know about computers and cost analysis."

Hunter chuckled. It was a deep, rumbly chuckle that started in his chest and worked upward to create a hundred-watt smile. A shiver coursed through Brenna and she managed a weak smile in return, then fiddled with the napkin on her lap.

"Computers are a fantastic invention," Hunter said. "However, they're very intimidating to a great many people. Why, I don't know. I compile my data, then feed the information into the computer to analyze it."

"What kind of data?"

"Anything and everything. For example, I could produce a spread sheet for you showing the cost factors in housing a dog the size of Cookie versus a much smaller breed. But since Cookie is obviously a favorite guest of yours, you probably wouldn't care."

"I adore him," she said, laughing. "He's with me more than he's home because his owners travel a great deal. He's so cute. Except when he opens the door and escapes."

"Talented dog," Hunter said, frowning in memory.

"I was so afraid that you were going to sue me. You're not, are you?"

"No," he said, smiling again. "I'm not."

The smile was shared as their eyes met and held. Before he was even aware that he had done it, Hunter reached out and took Brenna's hand. His thumb slid to her inner wrist and he could feel the wild beat of her pulse. Part of him was pleased that his touch affected her; another part could not ignore the increased tempo of his own heart as he gently stroked her soft skin.

"Your dinner," the waiter said.

The spell was shattered, and Hunter jerked his hand away.

"Fine," he said. "Brenna, would you like to finish your salad with your meal?"

"What? Oh, no, thank you."

A jumble of thoughts rolled through Hunter's mind, and he was only vaguely conscious of the taste of his filet mignon. Brenna was jarring him, throwing him off balance, and he didn't like it. When he had gazed into her chocolate-brown eyes he had felt a coiling tension of need, of desire, deep within him, that was somehow different from a purely sexual urge. Emotions had threaded through the physical pull. Emotions of protectiveness, possessiveness, toward the curly-haired whisper of a girl sitting across from him.

No, he had never before met a woman like Brenna MacPhee. She was the most open, honest person he'd encountered. If she thought it, she said it. If she wanted to know, she asked. She passed no judgment on a father who had put his own wishes first. To Hunter, the MacPhee sounded selfish and cold, but to Brenna the man had simply listened to his inner drummer. Incredible. Brenna wasn't logical or realistic, but she really was incredible.

She asked so little of life, he mused. All she wanted was stability, the chance to stay in one place and know that if she left, it would be of her own choosing. She dreamed of marrying someday and having a child. He pictured her in the arms of another man and frowned. Would she share the passion he had felt when he'd kissed her with someone else?

"Hell, no!" he said.

"Hell, no, what?" Brenna asked.

"Nothing. I didn't realize I had spoken out loud."

"You looked like you were a million miles away. I guess being an intellectual, it's difficult for you to shut off your mind."

"I'm not exactly an intellectual. I just have a knack for figures."

"Oh, it's more than that, Hunter. Everything about your life seems organized. Even the length of your hair."

"Are we back to that?"

"Well, by wearing it short it can grow without becoming too long too quickly and, thus, you don't have to go to the barber so often. Right?"

"Well, yes. I don't have time to. . . . What else?"

"Never mind. You're getting crabby."

"I am not! What else?"

"Your clothes. They're nice, really they are, and obviously expensive. But I'm guessing, just guessing, you understand, that you own mostly dark slacks and white shirts. That way, you don't have to get involved in coordinating your colors, and it's much more efficient. Logical, you know what I mean?"

"You're making me sound like a weirdo, Brenna."

"Don't be silly. I highly admire someone who has such total control over every aspect of his life. I try to get organized, but I never quite make it. I drive my accountant crazy. I run the Pet Palace like a champ, but beyond that I'm hopeless. I can see where it might be beneficial to dress like you do.

You should have seen me trying to find this shawl tonight. It was in my linen closet with the towels."

"It was? Why?"

"Because it's pink, and I put it with my pink towels. That was when I was on my organizing-by-color binge, but that didn't work very well either. You know, I'm surprised you haven't grown a beard. Think of the time you could save by not having to shave every morning. Now *there* is a logical thought."

"Oh, man," Hunter said, rolling his eyes heavenward. "Brenna, I'm not that set in my ways. Granted, I like order in my life, but I'm flexible, open-minded." Wasn't he? he asked himself. Sure he was. Wasn't he? Why was he having this insane conversation in the first place? "Let's change the subject. You're making me feel like an eccentric or something."

"Oh. Sorry. Okay, new topic. How come you still have a tan in the fall?"

"I run three-point-eight miles a day. I worked out a program and ran it through my computer to determine the most beneficial type and amount of exercise for a healthy male of my height, weight, and age. Hence, I run that distance every day, and I guess that's enough to keep my tan from the summer."

Brenna leaned slightly toward him. "Did you ever get totally reckless and run four miles?"

He squinted at the ceiling. "No, not that I recall," he said. "It wouldn't serve any particular purpose to go farther. I have it calculated."

"Goodness," she said, sinking back in her chair. "Isn't there anything you do that you don't compute first? No, forget I asked. It's really none of my business."

"Your cheeks are as pink as your dress," he said, grinning at her. "Were you referring to sex?"

"Don't be absurd," she said, concentrating on her fish. "I have no intention of discussing your sex life."

"Oh, well, would you prefer to discuss *your* sex life?"

"Hunter Emerson!"

"Brenna MacPhee!" he said, chuckling softly.

Her name, Brenna thought dreamily, when spoken by Hunter wasn't a mere name. It was a celebration of sound, a— Oh, for Pete's sake, how dumb!

"I should check the national data banks with my computer modem," Hunter said, "and see if there're any statistics on the modern-day woman who still blushes. It would be a fascinating study."

"You might also check to see," Brenna said, ever so sweetly, "what information is available on how drastically the appearance of a handsome man is altered when his nose is broken."

Hunter whooped in delight.

Brenna sniffed indignantly, then her laughter mingled with Hunter's. For the remainder of the meal they tried to outdo each other in outlandish statistical information they should gather that would dazzle the country when disclosed.

Hunter never seemed to stop smiling and Brenna's gaze never strayed far from his face. She was having a lovely evening with Hunter, and was quick to agree when he suggested they have after-dinner coffee.

He was having a good time, Hunter realized, as

he stirred his coffee. He couldn't remember when he'd been so relaxed, had laughed so much. The really amazing part was that his mind hadn't strayed once to the project he was presently working on. Usually during a date he became bored with female chatter, plastered a pleasant expression on his face, and concentrated on his latest assignment.

But not tonight. Not while sitting across the table from Brenna MacPhee. And as he looked at her in the gentle glow of the candlelight, he knew she didn't play the singles game like the women he associated with. Brenna MacPhee didn't sleep around, nor dress and act for society at large. She was Brenna, who had her own kind of class, who was refreshingly open and honest, who made him laugh right out loud.

And Hunter desired her like no woman before.

The need was there, deep within him, building, causing his blood to pound through his veins. The sweet warmth of his sugared coffee reminded him of the sweet warmth of Brenna's mouth moving under his. The passion she had kindled within him was still a glowing ember, waiting to be fanned to a roaring flame.

Oh, yes, he wanted her, and it wasn't logical or reasonable, Hunter told himself. He had a sneaking, disturbing thought that having sex with Brenna would not be simply a mutually gratifying physical release of tension. Emotions would be involved. Dangerous emotions that he had neither the time nor the inclination to entertain. This curly-haired gypsy was, indeed, weaving some unearthly spell over him and it had to stop. Now!

"Well, it's getting late," he said abruptly, "and tomorrow is a work day. Are you ready to go?"

"Oh, yes, of course," she said, looking at him in surprise.

The night had become unusually warm and the sky was an umbrella of twinkling stars. Brenna filled her lungs with the clean air.

"What a beautiful sky," she said, gazing up at the heavens. "I feel as though I could just pluck one of those stars for my very own."

"And what would you do with it?" Hunter asked, smiling in spite of himself.

"Make a wish."

"What kind of wish?"

"Oh, I can't tell you, or it wouldn't come true. That's the rule about wishes."

"I didn't know that. Brenna, we're about sixth in line here for the valet to get the car. Would you like to walk through that little park across the street?" What? he asked himself. What had happened to taking her straight home and ending this evening?

"Yes, that sounds very nice," Brenna said, smiling up at him.

This was not smart, Hunter thought as they walked across the street. His actions didn't make sense, didn't follow his reasoning. Damn!

In the park, Brenna slipped off her shoes and wiggled her toes in the carpet of grass, delighted that it was dry in spite of the earlier rains. Hunter silently admitted defeat and laced his fingers through hers as they strolled leisurely among the stately trees. The bright half-moon and stars cast a silvery luminescence over the wooded area. A night owl hooted somewhere in the distance.

"Oh, it feels like velvet," Brenna said, sinking onto the thick grass beneath a tree.

"You'll get grass stains on your clothes," Hunter said.

"I don't care. Come sit." She patted the ground next to her.

"On the ground?"

"You can sit on my shawl if you like."

"No, I'll rough it, I guess."

He lowered himself and sat stiffly beside her, appearing as though he didn't know quite what to do with his long arms and legs.

"No good, huh?" she said, frowning.

"It's been a great many years since I've sat on the ground under a tree."

"Don't you ever go on picnics?"

"No."

"Why not?"

"I don't have time for that sort of thing," he said gruffly. "Consulting firms don't run themselves, Brenna. It's a highly competitive field, and I have to stay one step ahead of the other outfits."

"Yes, I suppose you do," she said, sighing. "I just think it's a shame, though, that you don't have time for picnics, and ice cream cones, and wiggling your toes in the grass. Don't you ever get tired, Hunter? Tired of working so very hard?"

"No," he growled, then, "Yes, dammit, I do!" and brought his mouth down hard on hers.

Three

Brenna's eyes widened at the rough onslaught of Hunter's mouth, but as the embrace softened her eyes drifted closed. He circled her shoulders with his arm and pressed her gently down onto the grass, his lips never leaving hers as he stretched out next to her. She laced her arms around his neck, drawing him closer. His tongue delved deep into her mouth, bringing an involuntary moan of pleasure from her.

With an arm about her waist he pulled her partially beneath him, one leg pinning both of hers in place. His lips left hers to trail kisses over her face, down her slender neck, across the soft skin of her shoulders. His arousal pressed hard against her, full and heated, a bold announcement of his masculinity.

He murmured her name in a dark, velvety voice and his hand brushed away the shawl, then skimmed over her breasts. His mouth sought hers again, and as he drank of her sweetness, Brenna felt herself floating away to a place she had never been. Passion stirred deep within her, then swirled throughout her. She sank her hands into his thick hair, urging him closer, savoring the sensations pouring through her.

She moved her hips upward, pressing against Hunter's straining manhood. He groaned deep in his chest, and she felt him shudder with desire, his muscles trembling as he strove for control.

"Brenna," he gasped, then rolled away from her. He sat up, crossing his arms over his knees and resting his forehead on his tightly clenched fists.

She struggled to sit up, pulling her shawl around her with shaking hands.

"I'm sorry," he said, slowly lifting his head but not looking at her. "I shouldn't have done that. Give me a minute to . . . I'll take you home."

"Why are you sorry, Hunter?"

"Are you crazy?" he snapped, turning to face her. "In another minute I would have taken you right here on the damn ground. I have never, *never* desired anyone the way I do you. You are driving me right out of my mind. I fully intended to see you home as soon as we'd eaten, but did I? Hell, no. I behaved like some horny kid in the back seat of a car. Dammit, what is it about you? You really are a gypsy, right? With spells and potions and— See? I'm cracking up!"

A bubble of laughter escaped from Brenna's lips, and she clamped her hand over her mouth.

"What in the hell is so funny?" Hunter roared.

"Nothing. Oh, Hunter." She placed her hand on his back. "Who are you angry with? Yourself or me? I've never felt the way I do when you kiss me.

It's wonderful. You make me feel special, beautiful, cherished. You can be sorry if you want, but I refuse to be."

"You're incredible," he said huskily. "You should be mad as hell, and there you sit with the moonlight pouring over you looking as serene as a madonna. Brenna, I can't handle this."

"What do you mean?"

"My mind is mush! I tell myself one thing in regard to you, then do the opposite. You operate on a different wavelength than I do. Your world encompasses picnics, ice cream cones, unicorns, and secret wishes on stars. There's no place in my life for any of that, or for commitments or long-term relationships. I don't make promises I don't intend to keep. I don't make promises at all. I'd take from you, Brenna, but I wouldn't give you a damn thing in return."

"I see," she whispered.

"I'll take you home now," he said, getting to his feet in a fluid motion and extending his hand to her.

He pulled her up next to him, then lifted her hand to press his lips to the palm. Sudden tears misted Brenna's eyes. A feeling of loss rushed over her, as if she had been a breath away from an elusive treasure and now it was lost to her forever. Hunter had evoked tempestuous emotions within her body and, yes, within her heart, soul, and mind as well. A new and wondrous world was just beyond her and she wanted to explore its gifts and mysteries. But only with this man. Only with Hunter.

They walked back to the restaurant in silence with Brenna's hand held tightly in Hunter's. She felt like a child, who had ventured where she didn't belong and was being led back to her own limited world. In the car she sat with her hands clutched tightly in her lap, willing herself not to cry. When she looked at Hunter from beneath her lashes, she saw him gripping the steering wheel with such force his knuckles were white. The tension virtually crackled in the air, and the pounding of Brenna's heart echoed in her ears.

"I'll see you in," Hunter said quietly when he stopped in front of her house.

"No, that isn't necessary."

"I'll see you in," he repeated through clenched teeth.

In the downstairs living room, Brenna snapped on the light and turned to face Hunter. Their gazes met, and Hunter saw the tears clinging to Brenna's lashes.

"Oh, hell," he said, then reached out and pulled her roughly into his embrace.

She circled his waist with her arms and leaned her head on his chest, hearing the thundering of his heart. He held her tightly, one hand at the back of her head, as if he would never let her go. Minutes passed, and still they stood there, wrapped in the pleasure of being together.

"Something happens to me when I'm with you, Brenna," Hunter finally said quietly, not loosening his hold on her. "Nothing makes sense. All I know is, you're very different, very special and rare, and I'm not prepared to deal with all the unknowns you bring into my life. I have a sick feeling in the pit of my stomach that I'd end up hurting you, and I'd never want to do that."

"Oh, Hunter."

"The things you need, I can't give you, don't you see?"

"We just met. How can you possibly know what I need?"

"I know, I really do. My work is my life, and everything else takes second place. You deserve better than that."

"So do you," she said, gripping the lapels of his jacket.

"No, Brenna, I have things in the order I want them. All my energies have to be directed toward my company, because it's going to be the best of its kind."

"That's very logical thinking," she said miserably.

"Yeah," he said, sounding none too happy either.

"I really don't think it's fair that you're deciding what I need or don't need."

"It's not?"

"No."

"Look, once you sleep on it, think it through, you'll realize that I'm right. I *would* like to know that you understand what I've said. I'll call you tomorrow."

She sighed. "Okay."

"Good night, Brenna," he said, then kissed her on the forehead. "Lord, there's a guinea pig sitting on my foot."

Brenna reached down and scooped up the furry animal, nestling it against her cheek. Hunter gazed at her for a long moment, then turned and walked out the door, closing it quietly behind him.

"Darn," Brenna said to the animal. "That didn't

go very well. But then again, Hunter *is* going to call me tomorrow."

She gave the guinea pig a loud, smacking kiss on the nose, then turned and headed for the stairs, a bright smile on her face.

When Hunter telephoned the next evening, Cindy informed him that Brenna had gone out with a group of friends to a poetry reading. The following night Brenna was home when Hunter called, and she told him in an excited rush of words how talented the newly discovered poet was. During the lengthy conversation that followed they debated the merits of various poets and novelists.

The next two nights they talked on the telephone for over an hour discussing favorite movies, the political scene in Portland, their predictions for Mount Saint Helen's, and a multitude of other topics. They laughed and shared, argued good-naturedly, and hung up with softly spoken good-byes. The issue of their relationship, Brenna decided, had been placed on hold.

On the fifth night after their dinner date, Hunter kept the phone call short, asking Brenna if she'd like to go to a movie the next evening. She agreed, but the subdued tone of Hunter's voice caused a knot to tighten in her stomach.

This was it, she told herself. Hunter was going to take his stand again on why he had no room for her in his life. Their long talks on the phone had given her a wonderful insight into who he was, his likes and dislikes. She felt as though she'd known him for a lifetime, and she didn't want him to walk away from her.

The next night Brenna's heart sank when Hunter picked her up. He spoke pleasantly with

Cindy, but grew tense as he and Brenna left the house. She was unable to concentrate on the movie, dreading what Hunter would say when they returned to the Pet Palace. She declined his offer of stopping for dessert, and they drove home in silence.

In the downstairs living room of the Pet Palace, Hunter stared at the Boston fern as if it were the most fascinating thing he had ever seen. Brenna waited, her hands held behind her back to hide their trembling.

"Brenna, we have to talk," Hunter said finally, turning to face her.

"Yes, I suppose we do," she said.

"I—"

"Brenna! Brenna! Brenna!" Cindy yelled, running down the stairs. "I tried to wait longer in case you guys were into something hot and heavy down here, but . . . oh, my gosh, Brenna, I think Darth Vader is having her babies!"

"Who?" Hunter asked.

"She's not due for a week," Brenna said, running toward the stairs.

"Try telling *her* that," Cindy said.

"Darth Vader?" Hunter repeated.

"Darth Vader Donaldson," Brenna said, hesitating a moment to look at him. "Mrs. Donaldson's cat. She assured me she'd be back from vacation before Darth Vader gave birth." She shrugged, then followed Cindy quickly up the stairs.

"Go home, Emerson," Hunter said to himself. "Open the door, walk out, and go home!" He started for the door, then muttered, "Oh, hell," and sprinted up the stairs two at a time.

Hunter caught up with Brenna just as she entered the second bedroom upstairs. Cindy was hopping from one foot to the other and wringing her hands.

"See, Brenna?" Cindy said. "Darth Vader is pacing, and whining, and— Oh, why don't cats take birth control pills?"

"What is all this stuff doing in here?" Brenna asked.

"That's clean sheets and towels," Cindy said. "And those four pans have hot water in them. Well, it was hot, but it's probably cold by now. Oh, Brenna, I didn't know what to do! Aren't you supposed to boil water when babies are born?"

"They always do it in the movies," Hunter said, nodding.

"You did just fine, Cindy," Brenna said. "Why don't you go on home and I'll take over."

"Don't you want me to reheat the water first?" Cindy asked.

"I'll stay and help Brenna," Hunter said. "You've had enough for one evening, Cindy."

"Yes, Cindy, you go on home," Brenna said, giving her a quick hug. "You did a wonderful job."

"I'm exhausted, just wiped out!" Cindy said. "Cookie is pouting because I wouldn't let him out of your living room. Do you think he'll forgive me? I swear, Darth Vader, you'd think you could use a little sexual restraint. This is a fine howdy-do you've gotten us all into. I'll call you tomorrow, Brenna, and see how this nightmare ended."

"Okay, Cindy. Good night."

"I'll see you to your car," Hunter said.

"Really?" Cindy said. "Would you consider having yourself cloned so I could have one of you,

Hunter? Hey, I'm sorry I had to interrupt whatever it was I interrupted when you and Brenna were— What I mean is— Oh, ignore me. I'm on the verge of hysteria!"

While Hunter escorted a still chattering Cindy to her car, Brenna emptied the pans of water and folded the sheets and towels. Darth Vader continued to pace and yowl. The other two cats watched from their cages and appeared totally bored.

"Cindy is on her way home," Hunter said as he came back into the room.

"Thank you very much," Brenna said. "I imagine you'll be leaving too. We'll have to discuss things another time, I guess."

"I'll hang around a while. What did you do with the hot water?"

"Cats don't need it," she said, heading for the door. "It would be best if we leave Darth Vader alone for now. She'll want to pick her place to have her babies, and she probably won't do it if we're hovering around."

"Oh," he said, following her from the room.

In Brenna's living room, Cookie was delighted to have company. Hunter pointed his finger at the exuberant dog, and Cookie rolled onto his back, paws in the air, tail thumping against the floor.

"I'll change out of this dress," Brenna said. "You know, Hunter," she added, laughing, "if things get tough, you can always be a dog trainer."

"Cookie understands me," Hunter said, looking rather pleased with himself.

Brenna left to change and Hunter pulled his tie off. He stuffed it into his pocket, then shrugged out of his jacket. Why was he still here? he asked himself as he undid the two top buttons on his shirt and rolled the sleeves back. He didn't know anything about cats having kittens. He should leave, get out of Brenna's way and out of her life. Had she understood what he had been trying to say to her the other night? Did she realize that he was wrong for her because he didn't have the time to devote to a woman like her? She deserved to be the focal point of a man's life, the most important thing in his world. Hunter *had* to think of his growing company first. He'd called Brenna every night with the intention of stating again that they shouldn't see each other, then had shoved the issue aside. He'd been caught up in Brenna's vivacious personality, her wide range of interests, and had thoroughly enjoyed their ongoing debates. But enough was enough.

Tonight was it, he told himself. The last of Brenna MacPhee. He'd figured her out, which was what he had intended to do. However, about the time he'd realized she was a very special woman, he'd lost control of *himself*. That would never do.

But, oh, damn, he wanted to make love to her. Each time he'd kissed her she'd responded more freely, and he had felt ready to explode. He wanted her with an intensity that was like nothing he had ever felt before. His mind and body were ganging up on him. But, no, he wouldn't make love with Brenna. It would be wrong, because she would come to him trustingly, honestly. He had meant what he'd said. He'd give her nothing in return. He was going to walk out of here tonight, and never see Brenna again.

"Nobility is hell, Cookie," Hunter said. "Why are you still lying there with your feet in the air? You look really dumb, kid."

"Well, let's check the maternity ward," Brenna said, coming out of the bedroom. She had dressed in jeans and a sweatshirt. She glanced at Cookie, and when the dog stayed in the same position, she shrugged and stepped over him. "Hunter, I really appreciate your willingness to stay, but it isn't necessary."

"That's all right. Just don't expect me to perform major surgery. What I know about cats is zip."

"Darth Vader shouldn't need us for anything. I've never seen kittens being born before, but I've read tons of material about it. It's exciting, don't you think?"

"That's stretching it a bit," he mumbled.

Brenna opened the door, then gasped as a furry black blur dashed in, ran across the room and over the top of Cookie's stomach, and disappeared into the bedroom.

"Well, for Pete's sake," Brenna said. "She's picked my bedroom? That wasn't on the list of available choices."

Cookie scrambled to his feet, lost his footing, and landed with a thud on his nose.

"Cookie!" Brenna exclaimed.

"You check the mother," Hunter said. "I'll check Cookie's nose. Come here, pal. Let's see what you've done to yourself."

"You're a klutz, Cookie," Brenna said, marching into the bedroom.

When Brenna returned to the living room, she laughed in delight. Hunter had an ice cube wrapped in a napkin and was attempting to apply it to Cookie's nose. The dog was more interested in licking the frozen treat, and Hunter was scowling.

"Who's winning?" she asked.

"I give up," Hunter said, popping the ice cube into Cookie's mouth. "Don't blame me if his nose swells up. So, what's ol' Darth doing?"

"She's taken up residency in the middle of my bed. I put a towel under her, and the look she gave me told me quite clearly that I'd been dismissed. Would you like some coffee or lemonade? Oh, I have a bottle of brandy I keep on hand for the MacPhee, if you'd prefer."

"Lemonade is fine. Doctors aren't supposed to drink when they're on duty," he said, smiling at her.

"Oh, I see." She returned his smile. "I only have that small refrigerator and a hot plate up here, but I could go down to the kitchen and get some cookies."

"No, just lemonade, thank you."

She walked into the alcove off the living room and returned with the drinks. Handing Hunter a glass, she settled onto the sofa next to him. Cookie curled up close to Hunter's feet and went to sleep, and a silence fell over the room.

"I had a very nice time tonight, Hunter," Brenna finally said quietly. "I didn't get a chance to say that."

"I enjoyed it too," he said, staring into his glass. "Brenna, do you understand why it's best if we don't see each other again?"

"No."

"No?" He snapped his head around to look at her. "Weren't you listening to me the other night? I explained it all very carefully."

"I realize that, Hunter, but it was all from your point of view. You have every right to choose not to see me again, but I don't necessarily have to agree with your opinion. You said you don't make commitments or promises, but I don't recall asking for any."

"Oh, is that so?" he said, his voice rising. "What did you have in mind? A quick roll in the hay, then you'd dust me off?"

"I didn't say that. I'm trying to make the point that I'm responsible for myself and my own actions. I don't need protecting, Hunter. I'm perfectly capable of taking care of myself. You decided what I need in my life, determined that you couldn't provide it, then announced you were fading into the sunset for my own good. I resent that. I have the right to have my heart broken if I so choose. You are not my father, nor my keeper."

"No, I'm not. What I am is a breath away from becoming your lover. And that, Miss MacPhee, would be the mistake of the century."

"Thanks a lot," she said, banging her glass down on the coffee table and standing up. "Then I assume that your kissing me was a mistake too?"

"Yes. No. Dammit, you're twisting everything around."

"I'm just gathering your logical data, Mr. Emerson," she said, planting her hands on her hips. "Oh, forget it. This is ridiculous. I'm going to check on Darth Vader."

Hunter drained his glass and set it on the coffee table. He'd tried to do the right thing, he thought, and what did it get him? A furious Scottish woman telling him where he could put his noble gesture. But she was beautiful when she was angry. Her dark eyes had flashed like laser beams, her goofy curls had bounced around her head, and her cheeks had been flushed. Absolutely beautiful.

And everything was all screwed up again. He'd never been in a situation like this before. He'd felt he was doing the decent thing, but he'd blown it. Now what in the hell was he going to do? He'd never been so confused in his entire life.

"Hunter!" Brenna called.

Immediately he was up and moving, barely missing stepping on Cookie's tail.

"What's wrong?" he asked, rushing into the bedroom.

"A kitten."

His eyes widened and his stomach lurched as he stared at the tiny, slimy creature that was receiving a very thorough bath from Darth Vader.

"Oh, good Lord," Hunter said. "That is the grossest thing I've ever seen."

"Here comes another one."

"Not in front of me it's not," he said, hastily exiting the room.

"This is the miracle of birth," Brenna called after him.

"Grim, that's what it is," he said, beginning to pace the living room floor. "Computers are nice. They do as they're told, and they sure as hell don't reproduce. How can Brenna stand there and watch that? Sick. Really sick."

"Number two just slid into home plate," Brenna yelled.

"Oh-h-h," Hunter moaned, clutching his stomach. Cookie opened one eye, peered at Hunter, then went back to sleep. "I hope your nose swells," Hunter said to the dog. "Men are supposed to stick together at a time like this." Cookie began to snore. Hunter uttered a very colorful expletive.

"Three!" Brenna announced.

"Sweet merciful heaven," Hunter said, rolling his eyes.

During the next fifteen minutes while Hunter paced the living room, there were no more news flashes from the bedroom. He resisted the urge to peek into the other room, deciding that with the way his luck was running, Darth Vader would purposely wait for his arrival to deliver another kitten.

Brenna finally appeared, smiling broadly. "That's the extent of her efforts," she said. "Three babies, and they're so cute."

"Wet mice are not cute," Hunter said gruffly.

"Oh, Darth has them all dry and fluffy now. Want to see them?"

"No! No, that's okay. I'm really not cut out for this back-to-nature business."

"Wouldn't you want to watch your own child being born?"

"Well, I . . . um . . . I don't know. I've never thought about it."

"As organized as you are, I'd think you'd want to see the finish of what you started. Of course, childbirth is a bit more graphic than the delivery of kittens."

"I can imagine," he said, as his stomach lurched again. "Could we change the subject?"

"Oh, sure."

"We need to discuss us, you and me."

"No, I don't think so," she said, sitting down on the sofa.

"Why not?" he said, sitting next to her.

"Because you don't discuss, you dictate. I could tell you that when you kiss me, new and wondrous things happen to me. I could tell you that I think about you when you're not here, and my heart does a funny little tap dance when you walk into the room. Your smile is enough to melt me right down to my socks, and I adore the color, although not the length, of your hair. Oh, I could tell you a lot of things, but it wouldn't change the fact that you're about to walk out of here and never come back."

"You think about me when I'm not with you?" he said, smiling. "Nice thoughts?"

"You're pushing your luck, Emerson. I've heard your spiel on how incompatible we are. It's a unique brush-off, but the bottom line is still the same. I'd appreciate it if you'd leave. My bed is occupied at the moment, and your person is sitting where I intend to sleep."

"You can't sleep on this thing. It's lumpy."

"Don't you dare criticize my sofa," she said, jumping to her feet. "Good night. Go. Now."

"No," he said, crossing his arms over his chest.

"What?"

"I'm not leaving until we thoroughly discuss this. It's an unsolved problem, and weird things happen to my metabolism or whatever when I haven't tied up the loose ends of something."

"I don't give a tinker's damn about your loose ends, Hunter Emerson. Go stuff all your data into a computer and leave me alone. You made up your mind about me, my needs, about us, and I had no voice in that conclusion."

"Maybe I was wrong about the way I handled that," he said, staring at the ceiling. "It certainly seemed logical at the time."

"Take your logic and—and leave my house."

"Please, Brenna, let's talk this through like reasonable adults."

"I don't feel reasonable," she said, tears suddenly

filling her eyes. "I'm tired, and confused, and I'd really like you to leave."

Hunter frowned as he looked at her, and his heart seemed to clench when he saw the tears shimmering in her eyes. He pushed himself to his feet and picked up his jacket.

"Okay," he said quietly. "I guess any of those thoughts you might have about me after I go would earn me a spot on somebody's hit list. I certainly screwed things up, and I'm not even sure what I did wrong. I approached this thing in the same manner I tackle everything else but . . . I'm sorry, Brenna. Good night."

"Good night, Hunter," she said softly. "Thank you for staying while Darth Vader had her babies."

"Big help I was. I nearly passed out."

Their eyes met and held for a long moment. A moment that seemed to draw them closer together, as though invisible silken threads were weaving around them, pulling them to each other. But neither moved. A single tear slid down Brenna's cheek and Hunter took a deep, shuddering breath, then turned to the door.

He was gone. With a quiet click of the latch that seemed to echo through the silent room and beat against Brenna's temples, Hunter was gone. She felt empty, drained, and incredibly alone, and she allowed the tears to flow unchecked.

Hunter was in his living room with a glass in one hand and a bottle of expensive Scotch in the other. He was slouched on the sofa, his shirt unbuttoned and loose from his slacks. He had been drinking steadily since arriving home two hours before, and was still waiting for the liquor to numb his senses and blur his mind.

Instead, he was tense, filled with restless energy. The image of Brenna MacPhee kept dancing before his eyes. He saw her smile, heard her laughter. He could feel again her lips pressed against his, the firmness of her small breasts, the gentle curves of her body as it molded to his. His manhood stirred and he ached with need for her. Brenna MacPhee was like no woman he had ever known, and he was shaken to the very recesses of his soul.

So where had all his grand nobility come from? he wondered, draining his glass. Brenna was an adult capable of making her own decisions. She had wanted him, he was sure of it. And there he had sat, telling her how wrong he was for her, how their worlds, their hopes and dreams, didn't mesh. Why in the hell had he done that?

And why in the hell was he questioning his very logical, well-thought-out decision? He had begun to wonder if he were doing the right thing before he'd even left her house. Had the shock of watching Darth Vader doing her thing short-circuited his brain? Was this simply a momentary lapse in his logical reasoning? If he took two aspirin and called himself in the morning, would he find that he was once more fine, in dandy mental shape?

Lord, he hoped so, because right now he missed Brenna, could not erase from his memory the sight of her tears. How was it possible that such a tiny person could throw him for such a loop?

"Hell, I don't know," he said, refilling his glass. "I guess because . . . she's Brenna." Good. That hadn't made a bit of sense, so he must be getting drunk. He wanted to get totally blitzed and pass out into a dark oblivion where there was only nothing, instead of the haunting images of Brenna MacPhee.

But the first rays of dawn were inching across the room before Hunter Emerson put his head back on the top of the sofa and slept.

The shadows beneath Brenna's eyes the next morning gave evidence of her snatches of sleep during the long night. She had tossed and turned trying to relax, only to give up and succumb to the image that was haunting her. Hunter. As though her memories were delicate pieces of china, she had tenderly relived and savored each one. She had remembered the rich timbre of his voice, his distinctive musky aroma, the wide set of his shoulders, and muscled tightness of his thighs. His thick, silky hair had slid once again through her hands, and his long, strong fingers had intertwined with hers.

Then she had remembered the feel of his lips on hers, his hands on her breasts, his hard body pressed against her. Desire rippled through her in a sweet hot pain, and her breasts ached for more of his touch, for more of Hunter. Hunter, the dedicated genius, who belonged to another world. Hunter, whose smile melted her heart, and whose caresses and kisses awakened her femininity and made her rejoice in the knowledge that she was a woman. It was as though she had waited a lifetime for him, and yet in the same fleeting breath in which he'd come, he had left her, telling her they were not to be.

"Why?" she asked aloud, staring into her mug of

coffee. Why had she been given only a glimpse of ecstasy, only brief moments of what might have been with Hunter? It was as though he were trying to protect her from himself by telling her all the reasons they shouldn't be together.

And that, Brenna decided firmly, made her angry! How dare Hunter treat her like a child? She was a woman, by gum, with more going for her than just breasts and— Forget that. She hadn't exactly been dished out a generous serving of bazooms, but still . . . Damn that Hunter Emerson and his superbrain, his logical, analytical reasoning. He was driving her right up the wall. And he was rather inconsistent, too, now that she thought about it. One minute he was blithering on like a computer printout as to why they shouldn't see each other again, and the next minute he was saying, maybe they should talk it over. The man was giving her the crazies! The man was also gone. Was that her fault? She'd been the one to send him packing, but he'd changed his mind so often, he'd probably have left anyway.

"What a bum," she said to Cookie. "No commitments, no promises, he said. Did I ask for any? No, I did not! I simply wanted to be with him, see that glorious smile, and be kissed until I couldn't breathe. He's stingy, Cookie. There he is, in that great, big, strong body with the most luscious lips and magnificent hands, and he won't even share. What a rat!"

Hunter stood under the shower and let the water beat against his body. He was dying, he thought. Dying! There was a jackhammer in his head pounding away with no mercy. Getting sloshed had seemed like a good idea at the time, but, oh, he was dying. He hadn't gotten nearly enough sleep, his muscles ached from the hours slouched on the sofa, his head was about to fall off, and it was all Brenna MacPhee's fault. Damn her and her big brown eyes, her lilting laugh, her body that fit so perfectly against his . . .

"Don't start *that* again," he said, stepping out of the shower. "Do *not* think about her lips and breasts and— Oh, hell!"

He dried off and strode naked into his bedroom. He'd made a very big mistake, he decided as he pulled on his clothes. He had backed away from the most desirable woman he had ever known because of some misplaced sense of right and wrong. No, dammit, he'd analyzed the situation and his deductions had been correct. He did not have room in his life for Brenna. So, why couldn't he just leave it alone, move on and forget her?

It was the headache. Yes, of course. A man couldn't be expected to operate on all eight cylinders when his head hurt. He'd have some coffee, then go to work. His trusty project would get him back on track.

Fifteen minutes later, Hunter left his apartment dressed in a dark suit and strode down the hall to the elevator.

"Damn it to hell!" he roared suddenly, and spun on his heel and retraced his steps.

He'd forgotten to put on his shoes.

Four

Hunter Emerson Consulting Corporation was made up of Hunter, Charley Alan, a brilliant man in his midtwenties, and Maggie Downes, their attractive, highly efficient thirty-year-old secretary. Maggie's frown greeted Hunter upon his arrival at the office.

"The mighty master arrives," she said. "Late. I was about to call out the Marines to search for you. You look terrible, by the way."

"Thanks," Hunter said, squeezing the bridge of his nose. "You're terrific for my morale."

"Are you sick or hung over?"

"I'm not sick."

"What?" she gasped, covering her heart with her hand. "Hunter Emerson, cost analyst extraordinaire, got blitzed? Will wonders never cease? That wasn't a very logical thing to do, my sweet. Want an aspirin?"

"What I want," he snapped, "is for you to put a

cork in it. I'm not in the mood for your weird sense of humor."

"Got it. Just one question. Why did you over-indulge, as the saying goes? I've never known you to do that before."

"I was pushed to the edge, Maggie. The very edge, I tell you!"

"By who? Or is it whom? Or was it a what?"

"It was," Hunter said through clenched teeth, "a Scottish Shirley Temple, a furry Cookie, and a Darth Vader, who shot the zero-population-growth concept straight to hell."

"Huh?"

"Forget it!" Hunter said, striding down the hall. "Just forget the whole damn thing!"

A half hour later, Maggie entered Hunter's office and placed a cup of coffee in front of him on the desk. He was slouched in his chair, sound asleep.

"Hunter?" she said, jiggling his arm. "Hunter, wake up."

"I'm awake!" he yelled, jumping to his feet and whacking his knee on the edge of his desk. "Ow! Dammit!"

"Hunter, you've got a tight deadline on that project for the hotel. I hated to disturb you, but you've got to get to work. Charley called in. Things are going fine at the florist. He has nearly half his data collected already. Are you with me?"

"Yeah," he said, dropping back into his chair.

"Want to talk about what's bothering you?"

"Maggie, I'm a wreck, a mental basket case. I met this girl— No, she's a woman, a beautiful, unique, lovely woman. Anyway, I couldn't figure her out because she's so different from the women I know. Then when I *did* figure her out, I knew in a flash I had to get out of her life, pronto. Fine, great. Except she won't leave my brain space alone! She's haunting me! I want to see her again, but I don't dare see her again, but if I don't see her again, I'll probably go out of my mind! *Oh-h-h*, my head hurts. My knee hurts too. But it really doesn't matter if my body is deteriorating, because my brain has already turned into oatmeal."

"My Lord," Maggie said. "In the three years I've worked for you, I've never seen you display so much emotion. And it's all because of a woman. Amazing."

"I should have kept my mouth shut," he grumbled.

"No, no, now that I'm over my initial shock of a female person getting to 'love 'em and leave 'em Emerson,' I intend to help you. What's wrong with this woman?"

"Nothing."

"Check. She's perfect. What's her name?"

"Brenna MacPhee."

"Check. So, whatsa prob? Go for the gusto with perfect Brenna."

"I can't," he said. "She's open, honest, trusting, has class, and doesn't sleep around. She deserves more and better than I can give her. Every bit of logical data I've gathered indicates we're wrong for each other. No, *I'm* wrong for *her*, pure and simple. She needs someone who'll put her first, who'll help with kittens being born in the middle of her bed."

"Kittens doing what?"

"Never mind. It loses something in the translation. Maggie, I'm married, so to speak, to this company. I don't have time to devote to a woman like

Brenna. Hell, she even goes on picnics and eats ice cream cones."

"How decadent."

"Maggie!"

"Sorry. Look, here's my opinion. You've worked so hard to get this company going, and it's doing beautifully. It's time for you to relax a bit, reap some of the rewards of your labors. You need to do more away from this office so that your life is better balanced. Charley is married, and so am I. Why can't you have someone like Brenna?"

"No!" he said, smacking the desk with his hand. "This is the Hunter Emerson Consulting Corporation. Owned by Hunter Emerson. And, by damn, my name is going to mean something in this town!"

"Super. Then don't see Brenna again. Who knows? Maybe she'll ask you to do a cost analysis when she plans her wedding. Marrying, by the way, someone other than Hunter Emerson, who's known from one end of Portland to the other."

"I . . ."

"Think about it," Maggie said, heading for the door. "Computers and spread sheets can't snuggle on a cold winter night. Are you really sure you know what you want, Hunter?" she added as she left the room.

"Listen for the drummer," he said quietly. "Oh, brother, what am I going to do?"

He worked. Like a man possessed, Hunter concentrated on the project for the hotel. At noon, he mumbled his thanks when Maggie shoved a sandwich into his hand. At five, he nodded absently when she said she was leaving for the day. At seven, he gave up the mental battle he was fighting, picked up the phone, and called Brenna.

"Pet Palace," she said.

"Hello, Brenna. This is—"

"Hunter?"

"Yeah. I . . . Um . . . How are the kittens?"

"Fine. I put them in a box with Darth Vader, so I have my bed back."

"Good. Is Cookie's nose all right?"

"Yes."

"Brenna, look, I still feel that you and I shouldn't see each other again, but I can't get you off my mind. I like being with you. The thing is, nothing has changed. I have to put this company first. If we had had a date tonight, I would have had to break it because I have a deadline. If I were you, I'd tell me to take a hike. I'm going to leave it up to you. Will you go out with me Saturday night?"

"Yes."

"That was an awfully fast reply. Wouldn't you like to think it over?"

"No."

"Oh. Well, okay. It's my father's birthday and we'll have to put in a quick appearance at his annual birthday cocktail party, then we can go somewhere else afterward. Eight o'clock?"

"I'll be ready. Will you call in the meantime? I really enjoyed our conversations on the phone."

"No, I won't have time."

"Not even for a phone call? You were at the office those other nights. Surely you can take a short break."

"I have to get this project finished. I just told you that."

"I know, but you have to come up for air. Don't I

rate even a—" She sighed. "Never mind. I understand that you have to keep your priorities straight. I'll see you Saturday night. And, Hunter? I'm very glad you called."

"So am I. Good night."

"Good night," she said, slowly replacing the receiver.

Hunter, she thought. He had been on her mind throughout the entire slow-moving day. She had thought of him, missed him, yearned to see him and be held in his strong arms. The Pet Palace, which had always been her haven, her home, had suddenly seemed empty without his vibrant presence, his deep voice. Even Cookie had appeared to be looking for his new friend.

She had gone over and over in her mind the events of the previous night, hearing herself tell Hunter to go. But as the day had stretched into an eternity of loneliness she knew she wanted him here with her. The growing intensity of her feelings for Hunter was both frightening and exhilarating.

Brenna wandered around the downstairs living room, absently checking the multitude of plants to see if they needed water. But she couldn't ignore the question whispering through her mind.

Was she falling in love with Hunter Emerson? Was love evoking the new and tempestuous emotions within her, the sweet, sensual ache of desire, the heightened awareness of her femininity?

And if it *was* love, had she chosen wisely? The man couldn't even squeeze a phone call to her into his schedule. Hunter, in his own way, was like the MacPhee, focused on his dreams and goals. While Hunter's quest was real and obtainable compared to the MacPhee's chasing of rainbows, Brenna knew she would still be placed second in the order of importance. But if the seed of love for Hunter was, indeed, growing within her, there was nothing she could do to stop it. She could only wait, and listen for the drummer.

"And listen carefully, Brenna MacPhee," she said aloud. "This could very well be the most important message of your entire life."

Thursday and Friday passed with agonizing slowness for Brenna. On Saturday, Cindy arrived at noon to babysit while Brenna shopped for groceries for herself, then drove to the warehouse where she purchased her supply of animal food. Cindy would stay through the evening while Brenna was out with Hunter, whom Cindy declared yet again was the best-looking hunk of stuff she'd ever seen, even if he did dress like an undertaker.

That evening Brenna showered, then pulled her dress from the closet. It was lace, yards and yards of white lace that she had found on a remnant table at a fabric store. Cindy had sewn it into a stunning creation. The dress was sleeveless with a scooped neck, and hugged the gentle curves of her body before flaring in soft folds from her knees to her ankles. Both she and Cindy had a sneaking suspicion that the material had been intended for curtains, but were pleased with their inventiveness.

She looked very nice, Brenna decided when she was dressed.

She was also nervous. She was nervous because

she was about to see Hunter again, and she didn't know what her true feelings for him were. And she was nervous because she was going to meet his parents. She had suddenly realized that she was to attend Hunter's father's birthday party, and had decided she'd been a dimwit to agree to go. What did a person say to normal, run-of-the mill parents? Her experience in that area was limited to communicating with the MacPhee, who was not exactly a typical father.

Oh, yes, she was definitely nervous.

When the buzzer sounded, Cindy yelled, "Do you want me to get it?"

"I'll go down," Brenna said, hurrying from the bedroom. She pressed the button to unlatch the front door and called good-bye to Cindy as she rushed past.

"Have fun," Cindy said. "Cookie and I are going to have a popcorn binge."

Popcorn was nice, Brenna thought as she started down the stairs. Popcorn was a very healthy snack too. Maybe she'd stay home and eat—

"Hello, Brenna," Hunter said quietly, when she was halfway down the stairs.

She hesitated, then slowly descended the remaining stairs, her gaze riveted on Hunter as he walked to the bottom to meet her. He was dressed in gray slacks, a light blue shirt, dark tie, and a navy blue blazer. He caused her breath to catch in her throat when she looked into his beautiful blue eyes. He was also talking to her, and she hadn't heard a word he was saying.

"Pardon me?" she said, halting on the last step so they were almost the same height.

"I said you look lovely," he said. And beautiful, and gorgeous, he mentally went on. But the material of her dress looked vaguely familiar. Of course! There were curtains made of that stuff in one of the guest rooms at his parents' house. He smiled. Oh, yes, Brenna was a delight. And if he didn't kiss her within the next three seconds he was going to blow a fuse. "I need to kiss you, Brenna," he said. "I really, really need to kiss you."

"That's nice," she said dreamily.

"I'm glad you think so."

He brushed his lips over hers as if sampling their sweetness, then dropped his arms to gather her close to the hard wall of his chest. Her hands lifted to his neck, her fingers inching into his silky hair. He claimed her lips, parting them and delving his tongue inside her mouth. The wondrous yearning began deep within her and spread throughout her, as she returned the kiss in total abandonment.

Never had Brenna felt so feminine and safe as she did in Hunter's strong embrace. His masculine scent was intoxicating. She clung to his shoulders, and they felt as hard as steel. His tongue dipped and dueled with hers, and a soft moan purred from her throat.

He lifted his head and drew a deep, shuddering breath. He cradled her face in his large hands and gazed down at her, his blue eyes cloudy with desire.

"I missed you, Brenna MacPhee," he said.

"I missed you, too, Hunter," she said, her voice unsteady. "I thought about you. Nice thoughts. Even Cookie seemed to be looking for you. I guess I was wrong about you only owning white shirts and dark slacks."

"Not really," he said. Not bad, he thought smugly. He'd kept up with her disjointed conversation. He was actually getting the hang of it. "I bought these clothes today. You made me realize I was overdoing my organizing thing a bit. A black and white wardrobe is pretty dull."

"You look wonderful."

"I was hoping you'd think so, because I did it for you. That sounds dumb, I guess. I buy myself new clothes and say they're for you. I should have brought you some flowers."

"The clothes say more than the flowers would have. Thank you, Hunter."

He hugged her and kissed her quickly, then smiled warmly.

"We'd better go," he said. "I hate to subject you to the madness of this party, but I really wanted to see you, and I knew I'd be working every minute until tonight. We won't stay at my parents' house very long."

"Won't your father be upset if you just rush in and out? After all, it is his birthday."

"No, he won't care. His megabucks buddies will be there, all of whom, according to my father, have dutiful sons who followed in their old man's footsteps. That's probably a bunch of bull, but he loves to jab me with it. I'm only making my obligatory appearance so my mother won't be upset."

"Surely your father respects you for how hard you've worked, and for the success you've made of your company."

"No," he said, his jaw tightening, "he doesn't. I was supposed to be a lawyer. He decided that the day I was born. He's never forgiven me for not following the plans he made for me."

"Maybe with time he'll—"

"No, he'll never alter his opinion of my work. He calls my computers those little toys I mess around with."

"But—"

"Brenna, do you honestly think the MacPhee will ever change? Suddenly settle down and stay in one spot?"

"No," she said, sighing, "I don't. I guess you have to love your father the way he is, just as I love the MacPhee."

"Yeah, well . . ." Hunter shrugged.

"You do love your father, don't you?"

"I suppose I do. Yeah, I love him. But I really don't like him much, Brenna. That may sound cold, but that's the way it is. Let's go get this over with, so I can have you all to myself."

"Excuse me," Cindy called. "Could you give me a rough idea as to how long you'll be kissin' and stuff down there? I made the mistake of telling Cookie we're having popcorn, and he's getting really antsy."

Hunter laughed. "We're gone, Cindy," he said. "The place is all yours. Tell my buddy Cookie to go light on the beer when he has his popcorn."

"I didn't know he drank light beer," Cindy said, appearing at the top of the stairs.

"Never mind," Hunter said, chuckling. "She talks just like you do," he whispered to Brenna as they walked to the door.

"Really?" Brenna said. "Do we have some sort of regional accent? Oh, Hunter, be careful. Don't step on that turtle."

"Got it," Hunter said, laughing again. It felt good to laugh, he realized, as they walked outside. A warmth like rich brandy had spread through him when he'd watched Brenna come down those stairs. Lord, he'd missed her. The need to hold her, to kiss her, had consumed him with an aching intensity. He was out of control in regard to Brenna MacPhee. He knew it, but tonight he didn't care. Not tonight.

As Hunter drove through the heavy traffic, Brenna had a constant smile on her face. Each time she glanced at Hunter, her heart danced a jig. He was devastatingly handsome in his new clothes. Clothes he had bought and worn for *her*. All the flowers or candy in the world wouldn't have meant as much as his buying that outfit.

And when he had kissed her she had been filled to overflowing with joy, and warmth, and desire. There, in Hunter's arms, she had become whole. The inner chill of loneliness had been pushed aside and replaced by sunshine. The message from her drummer was becoming clear. She was falling in love with Hunter Emerson.

She shifted in her seat and stared at him, missing no detail of his handsome, tanned face, his wide shoulders, the muscles flexing in his thighs when he pressed on the brake. An amalgam of emotions assaulted her. She felt excitement and wonder that this man had captured her heart, and then the tug of fear as she wondered where it would all lead her. Hunter didn't love her, had stated very clearly that his business came first. He would fit her in around the edges of his life, just like the MacPhee did.

With a quiet sigh, Brenna turned to gaze out the side window. She was in love, and a part of her was glowing. But another part of her held a lingering sadness because she was not loved in return.

So be it, she decided firmly. She couldn't change the course of her emotions, nor transform Hunter into whom she wished him to be. She had listened to her drummer, and would treasure each precious moment that she spent with Hunter Emerson.

"Clouds are rolling in," Hunter said, bringing Brenna from her reverie. "Maybe you should have brought a sweater."

"I'll be fine," she said, smiling at him. "I've lived in much colder places than this."

"It must have been rough moving so often."

"Yes, it was. That's why the Pet Palace means so much to me. It's the first real home I've ever had. But, Hunter, I learned to accept the MacPhee as he was. Accept and love him, no matter what." Just as she loved Hunter as *he* was, she added silently.

"You're quite a woman, Brenna MacPhee," Hunter said. "You really are. Well, here's the house. Let's get this over with. I'll park on the street so we won't get blocked in."

Brenna's eyes widened as she looked up at the enormous home set back from the road beyond a sweeping front lawn. She had paid no attention to where they were driving, and only now realized they were in an exclusive, affluent section of Portland. The house was brightly lit and expensive cars lined the circular drive and the street where Hunter parked.

"This is where you grew up?" Brenna asked as they walked up the driveway.

"Yep. My room was the second window upstairs. Messiest bedroom in Portland, Oregon."

"Oh, I doubt that," she said, laughing softly. "You're too organized."

"Ahh, how well you know me. Actually, it was part of a master plan. If I left my clothes strewn all over, the maid had something to do and didn't touch my other things, which were arranged exactly how I wanted them. Worked great."

The maid? Brenna's mind echoed. She'd assumed that Hunter's father was a successful lawyer, but she certainly hadn't expected wealth on this scale. And she'd been worried about conversing with ordinary parents? Forget that. What did a person say to a king and queen? No, darn it, it didn't matter how much money they had. She was a MacPhee!

Hunter placed his hand beneath Brenna's elbow as they walked up the wide front steps and across the porch. Carved wooden doors were swept open by a woman in a dark uniform.

"Mister Hunter," she said, beaming at him, "how good to see you."

"Hello, Annie," he said, smiling. He escorted Brenna into the tiled entryway. "This is Brenna MacPhee. I gather from the noise that the party is in full swing."

"Indeed it is," Annie said. "Your mother has been looking for you."

Brenna's gaze took in the twinkling chandeliers above, and the winding staircase off to the right. She wondered absently if Hunter had ever slid down the bannister when he was a little boy.

"See that bannister?" he whispered. "I slid down it once, flew off the end, and broke my arm. It was a great flight, except for the landing."

She laughed in delight, then noticed a woman walking toward them.

"Hunter, there you are," the woman said.

"Yep, here I am," he said, kissing the woman on the cheek. "Mother, I'd like you to meet Brenna MacPhee. Brenna, my mother, Charlotte Emerson."

"Hello," Brenna said, extending her hand.

Charlotte Emerson was tall and slender with perfectly coiffured gray hair. Her dress was a rose-colored silk that accentuated her lovely figure, and her eyes were the same sparkling blue as Hunter's. She smiled warmly as she took Brenna's hand in both of hers.

"I'm delighted to meet you, Brenna," she said, "and I'm so glad you're here. That's a marvelous dress."

Oh, no, the curtains in the guest room! Hunter thought, looking quickly at his mother.

"The material is so delicate," Charlotte went on. "I've never seen anything quite like it. It's lovely."

"Thank you," Brenna said.

Bless you, Mother, Hunter said silently.

"Hunter," Charlotte said, "you'd best go wish your father a Happy Birthday, then help yourself to the buffet. I really must mingle. I know you're going to scoot out as quickly as you can, but kiss me good-bye before you go. You look tired, which means you're working too hard. Well, at least I know you won't be going back to the office tonight, unless you're a total idiot."

"Cost analysis is the furthest thing from my mind," Hunter said, laughing.

"I should hope so," Charlotte said. "You're in the company of a beautiful young woman."

"Oh," Brenna said, feeling the warm blush on her cheeks.

"Enjoy," Charlotte said. "I must do my hostess duties. I never should have worn new shoes. My feet are killing me. By the way, Hunter, I love your outfit. It's about time you put some variety into your wardrobe. You always looked like you were in mourning."

"She's wonderful," Brenna said as Charlotte hurried away.

"Yeah, she is," Hunter said. "Ready to meet the lion in his den?"

"Your father can't be all that bad."

"Ha!" he said, and took her hand and led her into the gigantic living room.

The room was crowded and the buzz of voices and bursts of laughter reverberated through the air. Hunter made his way forward, although he was stopped often by people who greeted him. He introduced Brenna to those he spoke to, and she received absent nods. Hunter kept her tucked close to his side, and she jumped when he gave her a quick kiss.

"You shouldn't do that here," she said. "People will assume that we're . . . we're . . ."

"Lovers? I think that sounds absolutely perfect."

"Oh," she said, gazing up at him.

"Don't you think so, Brenna?" he asked, his voice low and husky. "Don't you think it sounds perfect?"

She couldn't speak as the air seemed to whoosh from her lungs. She was held in place by Hunter's gaze—a warm, tender gaze that made her knees tremble and her heart race. The room faded into a hazy mist and the noise dimmed to a distant hum.

Dear heaven, how she loved him! And yes, oh, yes, she wanted to make love with him. Her love for him had consumed her heart, her mind, and her soul. To receive his vibrant masculinity, the essence of him into her body, would be the completion of her commitment. To become one with Hunter would be a celebration, a joyous, wondrous union like none before.

"Brenna?" he said.

"Hmmm?" she said dreamily.

"Come meet my father."

"Who? Oh!" she said, snapping out of her trance. "Of course, your father. It's his birthday. Does he blow out candles on a cake? I adore blowing out candles and making a wish."

"Stars and birthday candles," Hunter said, smiling at her gently. "What else do you wish on?"

"Rainbows and four-leaf clovers."

"And unicorns? I saw your collection in your living room."

"No," she said softly, frowning as she averted her eyes from his. "Not unicorns. They're make-believe, a symbol of something that isn't really true."

"Hey," he said, tilting her chin up with one long finger, "you suddenly look so sad. It has something to do with the unicorns. Talk to me, Brenna."

"I—"

"Hunter!" a voice boomed. "Are you going to greet your father on his birthday, or not?"

"And now the lion roars," Hunter mumbled. "We'll make it a quick stop."

As Brenna and Hunter moved through the crowd to where four men were standing, Brenna had no difficulty recognizing the elder Mr. Emerson. His hair was the same shade as Hunter's, though it was also generously peppered with gray. He was shorter than his son, and a soft belly was beginning to protrude over his belt. But he had the same handsome, rugged features as Hunter did, and the resemblance between the two was remarkable. Brenna now realized that Hunter's mother had passed on to her son only her sparkling blue eyes. The father's genes had dominated when the son had been created.

Hunter made the introductions, and while Brenna smiled at each of the men, she could sense Frank Emerson staring at her. She turned to meet his gaze steadily.

"I trust you're enjoying your birthday, Father?" Hunter said.

"I suppose. It does, however, remind me of my age, and the fact that I'll be considering retiring soon. Of course, I could postpone it, if I was assured you'd be joining the firm and taking over in the future."

Hunter lifted two glasses of champagne from the tray of a passing waiter and handed one to Brenna. "Drink?" he asked.

"Thank you," she said.

"I understand your business is doing quite well, Hunter," a portly gentleman said.

"Yes, it is, Mr. Mercer," Hunter said. "I'm very pleased with the progress and the reputation we're establishing. Hunter Emerson Consulting Corporation is making a name for itself in Portland."

Brenna looked up at Hunter quickly. Had she imagined it, she wondered, or had Hunter emphasized his first name when he recited the name of his company? Yes, he had. He'd pronounced

Hunter slowly and distinctly, then skittered past the Emerson. And from the scowl on Frank Emerson's face, it had not gone unnoticed.

"I congratulate you, Hunter," Mr. Mercer said. "You're in a highly competitive field. It's extremely difficult to start a company from nothing and build it into a worthwhile enterprise."

"And totally unnecessary," Frank said. "Emerson and Emerson Attorneys was started by my father, then taken over by me. It's there, waiting for the third generation to step in."

"Which Hunter obviously isn't going to do," Mr. Mercer said, smiling. "I would have thought that you'd come to realize it by now, Frank."

"It's never too late for a person to come to their senses," Frank said tightly.

"But they must listen for their drummer," Brenna said. "That's our inner voice, Mr. Emerson. It's so important that we know who we are and what we need to make us happy."

"At the cost of others?" Frank said. "You're wrong, young woman. There are such things as duty, family honor, tradition. Fanciful whims cannot be entertained."

"Father, let's give it a rest, okay?" Hunter said wearily. "We've been over this a million times. I'd prefer to spare Brenna this nonsense."

"Nonsense!" Frank roared. "You're Frank Emerson's son and—"

"No, dammit ! I'm Hunter Emerson. I'm a grown man leading my own life. Oh, hell, I've had enough of this. Good night, Father." He grabbed Brenna's arm and began leading her back across the room. "Oh, and Happy Birthday," he added over his shoulder.

"Disrespectful pup!" Frank called after him.

"We're leaving, Mother," Hunter said, stopping in front of Charlotte. "Your husband was his usual charming self."

"Oh, dear, I'm so sorry," Charlotte said. "I always hope it will be different between you and your father, but it never is. You're both so headstrong and stubborn. And I love you both. Now, you take your lovely Brenna and go someplace fun. I'll talk to you soon, dear."

"You're a doll," Hunter said, kissing her on the cheek. "Good night."

"It was a pleasure meeting you, Mrs. Emerson," Brenna said.

"And what is known as an experience meeting my husband," Charlotte said, laughing. "Shoo. This is a stuffy party. Go find a romantic place where you can dance until dawn. Providing, of course, that your feet aren't killing you like mine are."

Brenna smiled and decided she definitely liked Charlotte Emerson. Frank was another story, though. How could a father be so narrow-minded and cold? she wondered. He should be bursting with pride over Hunter's accomplishments, but instead he was throwing a tantrum like a toddler who hadn't gotten his own way. And she had a feeling that Hunter was right. Frank Emerson wasn't going to change, no more than the MacPhee was. But what of Hunter? If he fell in love, could he, would he, put his life into a better balance, not always place his business first? Probably not. He'd heard his drummer, and the tune was clear.

Outside, Hunter strode with heavy steps toward the car, and Brenna had to scramble to keep up with him. His brows were knitted into a deep frown, and his jaw was set in a hard line. He stopped so abruptly at the car that Brenna bumped into him. He turned to face her as though surprised to see her there.

"Damn," he said, raking his hand through his hair. "I'm sorry. I never should have brought you here. I should have come myself, then stopped by for you later. I was being selfish, because I wanted to be with you. I shouldn't have subjected you to the hostility between my father and me."

"Oh, Hunter, I'm not upset by what happened. I'm just sorry that things are the way they are between the two of you. I just can't understand your father's attitude. But then, I suppose the MacPhee doesn't make much sense to some people either."

Hunter gathered her into his arms. "What's really important is whether you and I understand each other," he said, his voice low. "Oh, Brenna MacPhee, I want to kiss you right here."

"Then do it, Hunter Emerson," she said, circling his neck with her arms. "Just kiss the living daylights out of me, because I want to kiss you too." And she wanted to make love with him, her mind whispered. This was Hunter, the only man she had ever loved.

He slowly lowered his head and touched his mouth to hers. His tongue parted her lips and thrust inside as if seeking the path to her soul. She molded against him, her tongue meeting his, her breasts crushed to his chest.

A tight knot of need, of raging desire, coiled in Hunter's stomach. The groan that came from his chest echoed in his ears, and he reluctantly lifted his head.

"Brenna," he said, his lips close to hers, "we have to go to dinner, or dancing, or something. Right now!"

"Would you . . ." she began, then waited a moment until her breathing steadied, "like to come to my place for some popcorn?"

"I'm crazy about popcorn," he said, then trailed nibbling kisses down her throat. "Nuts about it."

"Me too," she said. "Let's go home, Hunter."

Five

Let's go home.

The clouds had gathered densely overhead and thunder rumbled through the dark night. When they were less than a block from the Emerson home, rain began to sheet down. Hunter turned on the windshield wipers, and their steady rhythm seemed to pound Brenna's words against his brain.

Let's . . . go . . . home.

Such simple words, Hunter thought, yet they held profound and deep meaning. To Brenna, the Pet Palace was exactly that; her home. The only secure, stable place she had ever had due to the wanderings of the MacPhee. In her open and trusting way she was asking Hunter to go there with her, knowing that he wanted to make love to her. He'd offered to take her to dinner or dancing, but she had said, "Let's go home."

This was wrong, Hunter told himself. He should

head for the nearest restaurant, stuff Brenna full of food, stay in a crowd, then kiss her good night at her front door. He was getting in too deep with Brenna, was following his emotions and the urges of his body instead of his sharp, analytical mind. He was not the right man for her.

But the words "Let's go home" had filled him with indescribable joy.

He rolled the phrase around in his mind, then through the chambers of his heart, and it sounded and felt so damn good. He envisioned his empty apartment and saw nothing more than a cold, sterile dwelling. The nights spent sleeping on the sofa in his office evoked an image of loneliness. Brenna's Pet Palace rang with laughter and whacky excitement. Her mere presence transformed the shabby building into a haven of inviting warmth and immeasurable love.

Love? his mind echoed. Was he falling in love with Brenna MacPhee? Good Lord, no! He wouldn't allow it. No, sir. Love did not fit into his master plan, his logical, well-thought-out program for his future. Someday, maybe, there would be time for a wife, children, but not now!

So why in the hell was he still driving in the direction of Brenna's house? he asked himself. What kind of scum was he to accept her quiet invitation? She wanted him, and Lord knew he wanted her. But to take what she was offering would be so damn lousy on his part. She didn't have casual sex, and their union would have deep emotional significance for her.

And what about him? he wondered. None of his thoughts or actions since meeting Brenna had come remotely close to making sense. Was it possible that he, too, would lose his objectivity if he made love with Brenna? He was already slipping into an emotional place where he had never been, feeling possessive and protective toward her. The risk was too high. He wouldn't make love with Brenna MacPhee.

"It's really raining hard," she said, jolting him from his jumbled thoughts.

"What? Oh, yes, it is. It's a lot colder too," he said, turning into her driveway and shutting off the ignition. "I'll go up and buzz Cindy to unlatch the door. When I motion to you, make a run for it."

"Well, all right."

Hunter left the car and sprinted across the yard. A few moments later, he opened the front door and waved to Brenna. She slid out of the car and started up the drive. But when her shoes connected with the slippery bottom of a large puddle, she was suddenly airborne, and she landed unceremoniously on her bottom in the muddy water.

"*Aaak!*" she screamed. "Oh! Oh, just dammit! Oh!"

Hunter immediately ran to her and scooped her up into his arms. With powerful strides, he carried her into the house and kicked the door closed behind him.

"Are you all right?" he asked. Water was streaming from his hair and clothes.

"Cold," Brenna said, her teeth beginning to chatter. "Oh, yuck, I'm all muddy and . . . My dress is ruined!"

"Curtains wash," he said. He strode across the room and up the stairs. Cindy flung open the apartment door and stared at them with wide eyes.

"Hi," Hunter said, smiling at her. "You better take off, Cindy, while you can still get through the streets."

Brenna moaned. "I'm freezing."

"Bye, guys," Cindy said, running out the door.

"See ya," Hunter said. He carried Brenna through the living room and bedroom, then into the bathroom. He set her squarely on her feet in the shower.

"What are you— Oh!" she yelled as he turned on the water.

"No sense in getting your whole house dirty," he said. "Rinse your clothes, then take them off."

"Off?" she said, sputtering as she swallowed a mouthful of water.

"Off," he said firmly. "I'll make some tea. Do you have any?"

"Yes, but—"

"Clothes. Off." He left the bathroom, shutting the door behind him.

"Well, for heaven's sake," Brenna said, "this is ridiculous. Whoever heard of taking a shower with their clothes on? Dumb. Really dumb."

As the yards of lacy material became thoroughly soaked, they got heavier and heavier, and Brenna felt as though she were wearing a suit of armor. She tugged and pulled, and with a sigh of relief dropped the dress in a sodden heap on the floor of the shower. Her bra and panties followed, and she stood under the warm spray until the chill left her body. Finally she turned off the water and dried with a fluffy towel, then slipped on her floor-length pink velour robe. After tying the sash tightly around her waist, she towel-dried her hair, flicked a brush through the wild disarray of damp curls, and padded barefoot into the living room.

Then she stopped perfectly still and stared at what was on the floor.

Hunter's clothes. All of them!

Slacks, shirt, jacket, tie, socks, shoes, and, oh, Lord, underwear. Dark-blue Jockey underwear. There was a nude man in her house! Hunter Emerson was strolling around naked. Oh, dear heaven, she was going to pass out.

No, she had to calm down, she told herself. This wasn't just any man, it was Hunter, and she loved him. She knew what she had been doing when she'd suggested they come back to the house. As bold, even brazen, as it might seem, she had known what the words "Let's go home" had meant. Had Hunter understood what she had been saying? Apparently so, as he had already gotten rid of his cumbersome clothes.

Brenna took a deep, steadying breath, then walked downstairs to the living room. She hesitated at the kitchen door.

"Brenna?" Hunter called. "Is that you? Ready for some tea?"

Why was she so nervous? she wondered. Because she was in love with this man, darn it. Her limited sexual experience was just that, extremely limited. She suddenly felt young, naïve, and scared to death.

"Brenna? Come on in here."

"No," she squeaked, riveted to the spot.

"Brenna," he said, coming closer, "what is—"

"Oh, no." She gasped, and clamped her hand over her eyes as he walked out of the kitchen and into the living room.

"Hello?" he said, pulling her hand free.

"Omigod, a blanket," she said, letting out a long breath. "The man is wearing a blanket. Fancy that. Isn't that nice? It certainly is. Hi, Hunter," she said, smiling brightly.

He stared at her, then at the blanket he was wearing tucked around his waist, and back at her flushed face.

"Did you think I was naked in your kitchen?" he asked, grinning at her.

"Don't be silly," she said, brushing past him to enter the kitchen. "Hi, Cookie," she said to the wiggling dog.

Hunter followed close behind, still smiling. Brenna looked so cute in her fuzzy pink robe, he thought. Like a little girl about to be tucked into bed. Bed? Oh, no, no way. He wasn't going to start thinking about her in connection with a bed. He should have gone home while she was in the shower, but he'd wanted to make sure she was all right after her fall. His own clothes had felt like sheets of ice, and he'd found the extra blanket in her closet . . . Well, no problem. They'd have their tea, he'd stick his clammy clothes back on, and get the hell out of there!

As Hunter stood at the counter dunking tea bags into mugs of hot water, Brenna sank onto a chair at the table and watched him in fascination. His back was broad and tanned, and she could see its muscles rippling as he moved. She thought about touching his bare skin and her heart began beating wildly.

So beautiful, she mused, crossing her arms on the tabletop. Hunter's arms looked so strong and were dusted with dark hair. His waist narrowed

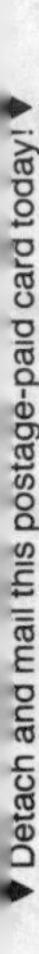
▼ Detach and mail this postage-paid card today! ▼

SEND NO MONEY NOW.
RETURN THIS
POSTAGE-PAID CARD TODAY!

where the blanket was tucked around him, and she could see a hint of his lean hips. He could have been chiseled from rock, smoothed, then bronzed in a warm, even color. Every rugged inch of him shouted his masculinity. Where he was hard and sharp, she was soft and curved, made to fit to his contours. He made her infinitely glad she was his counterpart, the woman to his man. So much strength in that body, so much power, and yet she knew he would temper it with gentleness when they became one. What had been missing from her life, had been found. Hunter. He filled the room with his vibrant masculinity, and filled her heart with love.

"Tea," he said, placing a mug in front of her. "Do you hurt anywhere from your fall?" he asked as he sat down opposite her.

"No, I'm fine," she said, taking a sip of tea. "It was very nice of you to rescue me. You've probably ruined your new clothes. We're going to make love tonight, aren't we?"

He nearly choked on his tea. "Well, I . . . No. What I mean is . . . Every once in a while I wish you weren't so straightforward. It's hard on my nervous system."

"I'm sorry, but it's just the way I am. We are based on honesty, aren't we, Hunter?"

"Yes."

"Well, then, I feel it's only fair that I be totally honest with you, and tell you that I've fallen in love with you. I do love you, Hunter Emerson."

Hooray! his heart sang. Oh, thank heaven, she loved him.

No! his mind yelled. He didn't want her to love

him. Love, to Brenna, was commitment for a lifetime, marriage. He didn't have time for all that.

"Ah . . . Brenna," he said, "are you sure that you love me?"

"Very sure. But it's not your responsibility, Hunter. I understand your need to concentrate on your business. I'm not asking you to change, or make any commitments or promises to me. I simply thought you should know how I feel."

"I'm not the right man for you, don't you see?"

"I suppose you're not," she said, frowning, "but it's too late to do anything about it now. I listened for my drummer, and the message was clear. Besides, it was time."

"Time? To fall in love?"

"Do you know how lobsters grow?" she asked, her voice trembling slightly.

"Lobsters?" He frowned. Did she have a screw loose? What in the hell did lobsters have to do with falling in love with him? "I don't understand, Brenna."

"Well, you see, a lobster can't grow when it's encased in that hard shell. So it searches for a place that it hopes is safe, and there sheds the shell. It knows it's time because it feels cramped, smothered, in the old shell. But no matter where it goes at that point, it's vulnerable, has to literally risk its life in order to grow. I'm growing and changing, Hunter. My shell is too tight and I need to be free, to move forward, even at the risk of harm or heartbreak. Some women may fancy themselves as beautiful butterflies, or delicate hummingbirds. But I see myself as that lobster needing, wanting, to grow, knowing it's time to love, truly love, a very special man. That man is you."

She sighed, and to Hunter that sigh was as deep as forever. His heart thundered in his chest, and his throat tightened. A tempestuous emotion he didn't understand assaulted him. He was shaken to the core by Brenna's softly spoken words.

She *was* like the lobster, he thought. And she had chosen him as her safe place, stripping herself bare and trusting him to treat reverently the love she was offering him. He was used to being in control of every detail of his life, but suddenly he was off balance, beleaguered by this strange, nameless emotion. He wanted to run, yet he also wanted to stay and hold Brenna in his arms. He was torn between a raging anger, and the urge to drop his head into his hands and weep.

"Hunter?" Brenna whispered.

Her voice caressed his name and stroked him, calmed and gentled his inner turmoil. Without realizing he was moving, he stood and walked around the table to pull her into his arms.

She looked up at him, and a moan tore from his throat when he saw the tears shimmering in her dark eyes. He lowered his head and flicked his tongue over her lips, feeling them part at his gentle insistence. Their tongues met in the sweet darkness of her mouth, as he possessed her in a kiss that was long and powerful. She slid her hands up his hair-roughened chest to his neck, molding herself to his muscled frame. Feverishly, urgently, the kiss intensified as their passions soared.

"Brenna," he murmured, and kissed her throat, cheeks, eyelids, then returned to her swollen lips.

His hand slid inside her robe to find her firm breast. The nipple grew taut beneath the stroking of his thumb. She moaned softly, leaning closer into him, feeling his hard arousal pressing against her.

He released her, but only to lift her into his arms. He carried her up the stairs and into the bedroom, where he swept back the covers and laid her on the bed. Rain beat against the roof in a serenade as he sat down next to her and braced his hands on the pillow on either side of her head.

His kiss was gentle, soft, sensuous. He held himself in check, his arms trembling as he strove for control. She lifted her own arms to reach for him, to draw him closer to her, but he sat up abruptly, out of her reach.

"No," he said hoarsely.

"But I thought you wanted me, Hunter," she said, her voice quivering.

"Dammit, I ache with wanting you! I have never desired a woman the way I do you, Brenna."

"Oh, Hunter," she said, placing her hand on his back. He jerked away, causing her to drop her hand.

"I don't know what's happening to me," he said, his voice gritty. "I could hardly wait to see you tonight, to kiss you. . . . But, Brenna, I don't belong in your world. You've worked so hard, obtained your dreams here at the Pet Palace. Yes, you are like a lobster. It is time for you to grow, to love, to complete the picture of your life. I'm still piecing mine together."

"I understand that," she said. "I'm not asking for more of you than you're capable of giving. I love you, Hunter. That love doesn't come with a list of rules or demands. Love doesn't work that way. Do you like being in my world?"

"Yes. Yes, of course, I do."

"Then stay, for as long as you can, when you can."

"Like the MacPhee does?" he asked harshly. "That stinks."

"We all have to listen for our drummer."

"Oh, Brenna." He turned to face her, and she could see the pain in his blue eyes. "You deserve better than this, than me. But I don't seem to know who I am when it comes to you. All my good intentions to leave you alone get tossed out the window. I deal in logical facts, dammit, and none of this makes sense!"

A warm glow started in the pit of Brenna's stomach and spread throughout her, bringing a gentle smile to her lips. Hunter was falling in love with her, she thought. He was! Of course it didn't make sense to him, because love was a very confusing emotion. Loving Hunter wasn't going to bring her the storybook romance she'd often fantasized about, but whatever time was to be allotted to her, she intended to fight for, by golly.

"You said you like it in my world," she whispered, "and tonight you're here. Stay with me, Hunter. Make love to me, and forget everything that's beyond the door. There's no one here but the two of us, and that's all that matters for now."

With a moan that seemed to tear from his soul, he claimed her mouth in a rough, punishing kiss. Then the kiss softened, became almost tentative, and Brenna knew Hunter was holding back, giving her one last chance to change her mind before they were both swept away by desire. She wrapped her arms around him, cradling the back of his head and urging him closer. His tongue found hers and drew it back into his mouth.

"Brenna," he said, lifting his head slightly, his voice husky with need, "I do want you so very much."

"Yes. Oh, yes, Hunter, I want you too."

A wondrous trembling began deep within her as he slowly removed her robe, kissing the dewy silk of her skin as it was revealed. His dark velvety voice swept over her, as did his lips and hands. He shifted only long enough to drop the blanket he wore to the floor, then gazed questioningly at her. She smiled serenely and raised her arms to welcome him to her.

"You are so beautiful," he said, kissing each palm before stretching out next to her.

Her breath caught in her throat as her gaze swept over his magnificent body. His manhood was a bold announcement of his need, his desire for her, and she felt no fear, no trepidation, only infinite joy that he would soon be hers.

"I love you, Hunter," she said.

"Oh, Brenna, Brenna."

Sensations of sweet torment swirled throughout her. It was a journey beyond her wildest fantasies. It was the crashing of wild waves upon the shore, and the flutter of a butterfly's wing. It was ecstasy. It was Hunter. He kissed and caressed her until she was writhing, calling to him to quell the raging flame of passion that threatened to consume her.

His lips and hands seemed to be everywhere as he stroked her slender body. He drew the bud of her breast into his mouth and she moaned softly, her hands roaming over his back, relishing the feel of the taut muscles moving under her fingertips. His hand slid to her inner thigh, then to the secret darkness of her womanhood, and he groaned his pleasure. A honeyed liquid heat swelled deep within her and spread like a wildfire. Her heart beat with the cadence of a thousand drummers, and a rushing noise echoed in her ears.

"Oh, Hunter, please," she gasped, a sob trembling in her throat. "I'm suddenly frightened. I don't understand what is . . . It's wonderful, but . . . Oh, Hunter."

"I'm here," he said. "Don't be frightened, Brenna. Don't be afraid of what you're feeling." He wanted it to be so good for her, he thought fiercely, striving for control. She loved him. This was *her* night. It had to be perfect!

He moved over her then, and smiled at her gently, warmly, waiting until the flicker of fear vanished from her eyes and was replaced by desire. Parting her legs with his knee, he moved against her and slowly, slowly buried himself within her sweetness. Brenna smiled. It was the most beautiful smile he had ever seen, and a lump formed in his throat.

With a soft sigh of acceptance, of awe and wonder, she lifted to meet the thrusting force of his body. She rocked with the motions of the ancient dance. The tempo increased as they moved as one, their hearts thundering, heat and sensations seeming to weave through each other as if they were no longer separate entities.

Hunter felt torn in two, acutely aware of the physical pleasure his body was experiencing, and nearly bursting with joy at the emotional intensity of his joining with Brenna. Never had he known such completeness. He was alive, whole, able to give as well as receive. He rejoiced in his masculinity as it brought him the sweet haven of this woman's body, and the sunshine from this woman's soul.

"Brenna," he gasped.

"Oh, Hunter. Oh!"

He felt the spasms rocketing through her, felt her tight grip on his shoulders, felt his own body shudder with ecstasy as he joined her in the place she had gone to. He gave her all of himself, then collapsed against her, spent, sated. On trembling arms he pushed himself up to gaze at her face anxiously, questioningly.

"Brenna?"

"I . . . Hunter, I—"

"Brenna, please! Talk to me. Tell me you're all right. Tell me you're not sorry or . . ."

"Thank you."

"What?"

"Thank you for the most beautiful, fantastic, the most magnificent event of my life. I never knew it could be like that, Hunter."

"Oh, my Brenna," he said, and kissed her deeply.

He shifted away from her then, and pulled her to his side. She snuggled close and he brushed the damp curls from her forehead.

"I'm the one who is thanking you," he said. "You were wonderful. It's never been like that for me, Brenna. We shared more than just . . . It's hard to explain. There aren't words to tell you. Sleep now. I'll hold you right here in my arms. And, Brenna?"

"Yes?"

"Thank you for telling me about the lobsters. From now on, I'll view them as very brave and beautiful creatures. Good night."

"Good night," she said, her lashes fluttering against her cheeks as she closed her eyes.

Hunter tucked the blankets carefully around her, then rested his lips on her forehead. He felt again that fierce possessiveness toward Brenna, plus a need to have her close, so close to him. And then there was that other nameless emotion that kept tugging at him. What in the hell was that?

He frowned, then pushed the distressing question from his mind. The lobster, he thought, smiling gently. Only Brenna could tell that story and turn it into a thing of beauty. Her voice had been a whisper as she spoke of her need to grow, to shed her shell, and venture forth to discover what love offered. What loving *him* offered.

Oh, hell, he thought, his brows knitting into a scowl. What was he going to do? The lovemaking he had shared with Brenna had been like none before. He wanted her again, right now, this very minute. And he wanted her in the days and nights ahead. Lord, he was selfish, as self-centered as the MacPhee. Brenna's father came and went as the mood struck, when his plans allowed a fleeting moment for his daughter. And Hunter knew he would do the same thing, fitting Brenna in when he could. He was such a louse, a real sleazeball, and he seemed powerless to stop himself.

Why was she willing to settle for so little? he asked himself. Didn't she realize how rare and wonderful she was? No, probably not. The MacPhee had always placed her second in importance, and she'd never known another place. And here he was, Hunter Emerson, scum of the earth, doing the same thing to her.

But he had no choice, he rationalized. His company needed his devotion, attention, and energies. Hell, it wasn't his turn to be a lobster and shed his shell, to grow and bring love into his life. It wasn't his fault that his timetable didn't match up with Brenna's. If she was willing to accept their relationship as it was set up, who was he to argue the point? Right? Right. Then why the ache in his gut and the chilling waves of guilt that swept through him?

Brenna stirred in her sleep and snuggled closer to him. He gritted his teeth as his body responded to her softness pressed so tightly against him. He sifted his fingers through the silky cascade of her curls and willed himself to relax. He had to get some sleep. He needed to check over the hotel project once more before presenting it Monday morning.

Oh, great, he thought. He'd have to leave Brenna early in the morning and spend the day at the office. He'd rather stay in bed with her and make love. But he couldn't because he had work to do. Work that was vitally important, would complete yet another error-free project, take him one step closer in his quest to establish his name as a first-rate cost analyst.

"Hell," he muttered.

The rain had stopped. The moon slid from behind a cloud and shone beneath the curtains on the window, casting an eerie light over the room. Hunter shuddered slightly, feeling as though he'd been transported away from the here and now, and deposited in an alien place. He tightened his hold on Brenna, inhaling her sweet scent, then slid his hand down her back. He welcomed the quickening of his body, the heat that caused his blood to pound through his veins, as it told him he was truly here, and Brenna was with him.

With a weary sigh, he closed his eyes and waited for sleep to claim him, to numb his senses and his mind. But sleep remained elusive, just out of reach. The bright colors of dawn were bursting above the horizon before he at last drifted into a restless slumber.

Brenna woke from a deep, dreamless sleep and wondered foggily why she was unable to move. Suddenly she realized that it was due to a warm arm that was resting beneath her breasts. Her eyes shot open and she turned her head. Her nose was only an inch away from Hunter's.

Hunter. Beautiful, beautiful Hunter. The morning shadow of his beard made his tan appear even darker, and his lashes were thick as they lay against his cheeks. Oh, how she loved him. What they had shared in the joining of their bodies had been exquisite. It had been a giving and taking, a coming together like none she had ever known before. Only Hunter could take her to that place of splendor. The future with this man was a hazy blur, a sea of doubt and unknowns. But now, at this moment, she was in his arms, safe, protected, complete, and she was filled with happiness.

"I love you, Hunter," she whispered.

"Hmmm?" he mumbled.

"Sleep, my love," she said, smiling gently.

As much as she wanted to stay nestled close to his warm body and be the recipient of his kiss when he awoke, Brenna knew that the occupants of the Pet Palace would be waiting for their breakfast. She slipped off the bed, pulled on her robe, and quietly left the bedroom.

An hour later, the animals had been fed, the dogs were outside in their runways, and Brenna was seated at the kitchen table sipping a cup of hot coffee. Hunter appeared in the kitchen dressed in wrinkled slacks and shirt.

"Good morning," he said. "I didn't expect to find you gone when I woke up."

"I had to feed my guests. Would you like some breakfast?"

"Just coffee. I'll get it." He walked to the stove and poured himself a cup, then sat down at the table. "How are you?"

"Fine," she said, smiling at him. "Are you planning on smiling at me once you've had your coffee?"

He chuckled. "Sorry," he said. "There's nothing wrong with me that a shower, shave, clean clothes, and my morning run won't cure. Don't take it personally. Brenna, about last night. I . . . Well, it really was wonderful."

"Yes, it was."

"You're not sorry, are you? In the light of the new day?"

"Of course not. I love you, Hunter. I couldn't possibly be sorry that we made love."

"Brenna, look, I know you've accepted the MacPhee as he is because he's your father. We don't have any choice as to who our parents are. But you do have a choice as to who you love, who you give your heart to, when it comes to the man in your life."

"No, I don't. When love happens, it happens."

"Yeah, right," he said, frowning and shaking his head. "Your drummer raps out one of his ever-famous messages. I don't think your drummer is your best friend. He picked you a first-class dud. I should be spending a fantastic Sunday with you, making love to you until we're too weak to move. But guess what? I'm leaving in ten minutes and going to my office to spend the day working."

"That's okay," she said breezily.

"It is?" he said, his frown deepening. "Well, thanks a whole helluva lot!"

"Oh, I'd love spending the day with you, but I have so much to do."

"Oh?" He stiffened slightly.

"It's Cookie's birthday. He's two years old today. I'm going to bake him a cake, and we're having a terrific party."

"Brenna MacPhee," Hunter said, "you are crazy, and I absolutely, positively adore you."

Six

Hunter collected the rest of his clothes, then kissed Brenna deeply as they stood by the front door. And kissed her again. And then once more. Her legs were trembling when he finally left the Pet Palace and drove away.

She sank into a chair, leaned her head back, and stared at the ceiling. She missed Hunter already, she thought. She wanted him to march right back in here and carry her off to bed, where they would make exquisite love. The fact that he was working was the pits. It was definitely a bummer that his attention would be centered on dumb numbers and computers that were smarter than she was. She loved that man and wanted him here, front and center.

"Feel better now?" she said aloud, laughing. "That was a very nice mental tantrum, kiddo." She was only human, she told herself. She understood and accepted Hunter's need to devote himself to his company, his dream. But there was no rule in the handbook that said she had to like it! Well, she'd indulged in some old-fashioned self-pity, and enough was enough.

But what about the future? she mused. Hunter cared deeply for her, she was sure of it. He was falling in love with her. But even if his drummer whopped him on the head to get his attention, then told him that he loved Brenna, he might still ignore the message and run the other way.

"Darn it," she said, getting to her feet. "Men are very hard to deal with at times." And *her* man, she added, was absolutely wonderful. There was nothing organized or preordained about the way he made love! He was unleashed masculine power, tempered with gentleness. He gave of himself totally, holding nothing back. The analytical superbrain didn't exist when Hunter made love. He was one hundred percent male! "Goodness," she said, as desire swirled within her. "Go bake a cake."

Hunter drove home, changed into his jogging clothes, then ran his three-point-eight miles. He blanked his mind and ran. Back at his apartment, he showered and shaved, then reached in his closet for his pants. Hesitating, he searched farther and found a pair of faded jeans he'd forgotten he owned. At the far end of the closet was the vast array of sweaters his mother had given him over the years for Christmas and his birthday. He selected a royal-blue crew neck, telling himself that since he would be alone at the office there was no need to dress formally. After consuming toast, cereal, and several cups of coffee, he drove to Hunter Emerson Consulting Corporation.

In his office, he spread the computer sheets for the hotel project on the table, picked up his hand calculator, and began the tedious chore of double-checking the rows of figures.

He lasted ten minutes. Soon the image of Brenna MacPhee was dancing in front of his eyes, transforming the column of numbers into a blur.

"Dammit, Brenna," he muttered, "go away. I'm a busy man here." No, he told himself firmly, he wouldn't think about her soft skin and silky curls. He would pay no attention to the memory of her body moving beneath his, the sound of his name being murmured in a passionate whisper. He wouldn't dwell on her enticing aroma or the sunshine of her smile. No, sir. He had work to do. He took another look at the printout in front of him, then threw his pencil down.

How did a person give a birthday party for a dog? he wondered. Would Brenna actually sing to the mutt and tell Cookie to blow out his candles? Probably. Could dogs blow out candles? Cookie was no dummy. After all, he knew how to open doors. Brenna's dark eyes would sparkle with excitement, and her laughter would tinkle through the air. The Pet Palace would be a happy, fun, noisy place.

"Check the report, Emerson," Hunter growled, but he didn't move. He just sat there envisioning Brenna, allowing her to take over his mind and heart, and feeling the uncomfortable evidence as his body reacted to his thoughts. "That's it," he said, getting to his feet and scowling at the papers.

He should think about this for a minute, he decided. He had, after all, rechecked the figures for the hotel three times before typing them into the computer. Then he and Maggie had proofed them together once they were on the green screen. It really wasn't that efficient to be using his valuable time going over, yet again, something he already knew was completely error-free. It would be more practical and logical to place the report in the binder and consider the project ready for delivery. His mind amazed him sometimes with its brilliance! The hotel report was a wrap!

Hunter put the papers in a binder, flicked off the light, and strode from the office, a wide smile on his face.

"Happy Birthday, dear Cookie! Happy Birthday to you!" the group sang, then cheered and applauded the guest of honor, who barked and wiggled in delight, his tail thumping wildly on the ground.

Hunter crossed his arms over the top of the gate leading to the backyard, and watched the noisy activities. The Saint Bernard, two poodles, and a dachshund were in attendance, in addition to six children, Cindy, Brenna, and Cookie, who wore a pointed party hat on his head.

Hunter's gaze lingered on Brenna, examining in detail her slender figure outlined to perfection in jeans and a raspberry-colored V-neck sweater. Her curls bounced around her head, and she looked like a delighted little girl as she clapped her hands.

Had the MacPhee ever given Brenna a birthday party? Hunter wondered. Had she ever been made the center of attention on her special day? Probably not. Brenna had missed out on so much as a child, and now, as a woman, was filling each of those voids in her own unique, loving way. She brought such joy to those around her, such warmth.

"Brenna MacPhee," Hunter whispered. "What in the hell am I going to do about you?"

As he opened the gate and stepped into the yard, she glanced up and smiled brightly.

"Hunter!" she said.

"The hunk is here, guys," Cindy said.

"Hi," Hunter said, joining the group. "This is quite a bash. Happy Birthday, Cookie ol' buddy."

"I thought you had to work all day," Brenna said.

"I finished up quicker than I expected. Mind if I crash the party?"

She walked to his side and slipped her arm through his. "I'm so glad you're here," she said, smiling up at him. "Oh, and I assure you that I have two cakes. One for dogs, and one for people."

"Did Cookie blow out his candles?"

"They were peppermint sticks," she said. "He ate them."

Introductions were made, the cakes consumed, then the guests dispersed. The dogs were led to the runways and the children waved their good-byes except for two dark-haired girls about nine years old. They were dressed in identical pink jeans and T-shirts, and it was quite obvious they were twins.

"You're twins," Hunter said, not knowing what else to say. Brenna and Cindy were stuffing a trash bag full of party debris. "Do you like being twins?"

"Guess so," one said, shrugging. "Are you Brenna's steady boyfriend?"

"I'm rather old to go steady," Hunter said.

"They're lovers then, Gina," the other little girl said. "That's the word for old people."

Hunter's eyes widened and he turned his head to search frantically for Brenna.

"You're not so smart, Tina," Gina said. "You don't know everything."

"Yes I do. You're Brenna's lover, right, Hunter?" Tina asked, sticking her nose in the air.

"That sure was great cake, wasn't it?" he said quickly.

"Yeah," Gina said. "Brenna makes super stuff. She said she's practicing for when she has kids like us. I told her she could have our baby brother, but my mom said no. Are you and Brenna gonna have a baby?"

"Oh, Lord," Hunter muttered, sinking onto a picnic bench.

"Tina! Gina!" Brenna called. "It's time for you to go. Your mother will be expecting you."

"Thank goodness," Hunter said under his breath. "Bye, girls," he added. "It was very . . . interesting chatting with you."

"Bye," they said in unison, then headed across the yard to the gate. "Thanks for the party, Brenna!"

"You're welcome! Cookie loved the ball you brought him. See you soon."

Brenna ran into the house and Cindy plunked down next to Hunter.

"Brenna will be right back," she said. "She went to check on the cats. I'll be leaving as soon as I catch my breath. That was an exhausting party. Fun, though. I'd swear that Cookie knew exactly what was going on. Don't think for a minute that

I'm going to hang around. I know you want to be alone with Brenna."

"Rumor has it we're going steady," Hunter said, smiling.

Cindy laughed. "How quaint. Do people still do that? I'd rather have a torrid affair, except I haven't had any offers. Oh, well, my day will come. Brenna says all I have to do is listen for my drummer.

"Hunter, look, it's really pushy of me to say this, but please don't hurt Brenna. She's the nicest person I know. You're a scrumptious-looking guy, who probably has more women than you know what to do with. Brenna is very special, you know what I mean?"

"Yes, I do," he said quietly. "She's very rare and very special."

"Well, I'm off. I just had to say that. I'm sorry if I offended you. See ya, Hunter."

"Good-bye, Cindy. And don't worry, you didn't offend me. The last thing I'd ever want to do is hurt Brenna."

"You're a doll. Bye."

Hunter pushed himself to his feet and walked slowly toward the house. Brenna inspired such love in people, he mused. She was so outgoing and generous with her laughter, and created a warm glow wherever she went. The children he'd met today adored her, and even Cindy, who gave the impression at times of being a bubblehead, was concerned for her well-being. Well, dammit, he didn't need a committee to tell him Brenna was a wonderful woman. And he had no intention of hurting her!

But what if he did? he asked himself. He'd been up-front about where he stood in their relationship. She knew the score. So, okay, she thought she was in love with him, but that wasn't *his* fault! He'd made no promises or commitments. But, oh, Lord, he didn't want to hurt her. He knew, he still knew, he should walk away from her right now. And he also knew he wasn't going to do it.

Brenna checked on the cats, blew Darth Vader and the kittens a kiss, then dashed into her bedroom to run a brush through her hair.

Hunter in jeans, she thought. Sexy, sexy Hunter in tight jeans and a blue sweater that made his eyes look like sapphires was almost too much to take! She hadn't expected to see him at all, and then he'd shown up dressed like that! Whew! She had to calm down or she might attack his body.

Why had he come back? she wondered. He'd been so adamant about having to work. Oh, how she'd like to think it was because of her, that he'd placed her first in his plans for the day. But, no, she'd be kidding herself and that was foolish. Hunter had apparently finished what he had to do and decided to drop by. She mustn't allow herself to read more into his actions than was really there. But what would it be like to be loved, to be the most important thing in Hunter Emerson's life? She shook her head. She had better accept the facts as they were and quit daydreaming.

She hurried back down to the kitchen. Hunter was just coming in the back door, and they met in the middle of the room, stopping about a foot apart and looking at each other.

"Hello, lovely Brenna," Hunter said. He slowly

lifted his hands and cradled her face, his thumbs stroking her cheeks.

"Hi," was all Brenna managed to say as she gazed into his blue eyes.

In seemingly slow motion, he lowered his head and brushed his lips over hers. The feathery gesture made her tremble, and she thought she would collapse. He drew a lazy circle around her lips with the tip of his tongue, and a moan escaped from her throat. Hunter's breathing became raspy as he, too, fell prey to the sensuous web being woven around them. When Brenna flicked her tongue over his bottom lip, his control snapped.

His arms slid around her and he crushed her to him. She molded against him, savoring his taste, his warmth.

The kiss went on and on in a sweet torture that heightened their passions. The heat from Hunter's body invaded Brenna's and flames of desire licked through her, blazing a trail as they went. She was swept away with an aching need that started deep within her.

Oh, how she loved him, she thought. How she loved this man!

He slid his hands down her sides and over her buttocks to pull her up against him. His arousal was evident as he nestled her to him, and he lifted his head to gaze down at her, his eyes smoky with desire.

"I want you," he whispered hoarsely. "I can't get enough of you, Brenna."

"Yes, Hunter," she said breathlessly. "I want you to make love to me."

He circled her shoulders with his arm and they went upstairs to the bedroom, where he pulled her close and kissed her deeply. Voices of warning screamed in Hunter's mind, but he pushed them away, refusing to listen, refusing to pay heed to the fact that he was once again taking from Brenna and giving so little in return. With shaking hands he removed her clothes. His gaze swept over her body.

"So lovely," he said, his voice strained.

He shed his own clothing, then gathered her into his arms, fitting her against him as their mouths met in a feverish, urgent kiss. He lifted her and laid her on the bed, then stretched out next to her. His hand sought her breast, then his lips followed, drawing the rosy bud into his mouth.

Brenna's eyes fluttered and she smiled as desire flowed like warm honey through her. Hunter's mouth and hands were instruments of pleasure—of ecstasy!—and he was doing these wondrous things for *her*. And soon, very soon, she would have all of him. His strength, his masculinity, the essence of him, would fill and consume her, and they would be one.

His loving attention was directed to her other breast, and she moaned softly, sinking her fingers into his hair to hold him to her. She moved reslessly under his foray, and felt his arousal hard and heated against her.

"Oh, Hunter," she whispered.

"Brenna," he said, and claimed her mouth in a long, powerful kiss.

He came to her then with a bold thrust that instantly carried her away to a place beyond time or space. Together they soared, clinging to each other, calling to each other, then bursting onto the treasured shore an instant apart.

"Hunter!"

"Yes! Yes, Brenna!"

And then they were still, lingering there, savoring the moment before drifting slowly back to reality. Hunter rolled onto his back and pulled Brenna close. Neither spoke. They had been one but were now separate, left to tuck away in the private chambers of their hearts and minds what they had shared.

She was so wonderful, Hunter thought. He'd never be able to find the words to express how he felt when they made love. It was so much more than just a physical joining. Some of the emotions that were intertwined he understood. But there was still that strange shadow of an unknown something that tugged at his soul. It just wasn't logical that he was unable to unravel the puzzle within him. He spent his life finding solutions to confusing problems. Damn, he didn't like being defeated by himself! He had to figure it out!

"Oh, I hate to move," Brenna said, stretching leisurely, "but I have a new guest arriving soon. A basset hound named Clancey is spending a week here. He's never been away from his family before, so I'll have to watch him carefully for psychological difficulties."

He glanced down at her and smiled when he realized she was serious. He had a mental image of her sitting up at night holding Clancey's paw, assuring him his family would come back for him. Yes, he thought, his Brenna was something.

After a searing kiss, they left the bed and dressed. Brenna smiled at Hunter as she took his hand.

"Come see Darth Vader's kittens," she said.

"They're so cute, and don't remotely resemble wet mice anymore."

He chuckled. "Okay, show me the crew."

In the cat room down the hall Brenna dropped to her knees beside the box and crooned softly to the kittens as she stroked their heads. Hunter hunkered down, glanced in the box, then centered his attention on the woman next to him. He couldn't resist the urge to tangle his fingers in the curls lying on her cheeks and neck.

"The kittens are nice," he said, his gaze riveted on Brenna.

She laughed and rubbed her cheek against his hand. "You're not even looking at them. Mrs. Donaldson is picking them up tomorrow. I'll miss my babies."

Brenna should have a real baby, a child, he thought suddenly. She had so much love within her, would maintain a home ringing with laughter for her family. Family? That child would have a father, who would be Brenna's husband, the man who had planted his seed within her and helped create a new life. Dammit, he didn't want another man touching her! She was his. He was going to protect her, take care of her, love her, and— No. He wasn't going to fall in love with Brenna MacPhee. And he wasn't going to be her husband or the father of her baby. His mission, his goal, was clear. His company was all-important. He didn't have time for a wife and baby. He just didn't.

"Yeah, they're really cute little buggers," he said, clearing his throat and pushing himself to his feet. Brenna smiled up at him, and he extended his hand to her.

Brenna placed her hand in his and allowed him

to draw her upward, close to his body where she was immediately aware of his heat, his strength, his special aroma. She gazed up at him, unconsciously running her tongue over her bottom lip.

He drew in his breath sharply, then his mouth came down hard on hers. The kiss was potent and left them both shaken. Hunter slid his hands down her arms, then slowly released her hands as he took a step backward.

"I love you, Hunter," she said, her voice whisper-soft. "Sometimes I just need to say it aloud."

"Brenna, I—"

"No, I don't expect you to say anything." She was interrupted by the ringing of the phone and ran from the room.

Hunter followed slowly behind, a deep frown on his face when he entered the living room. Brenna was just replacing the receiver.

"Oh, Hunter, guess what?" she said, her dark eyes sparkling. "That was the lady who owns Cookie. She and her husband have decided to stay in Italy for several more months. She asked me if I would keep Cookie as my own pet. He's mine, Hunter! All mine. Isn't that wonderful?"

"You bet," he said, grinning at her. "Cookie is great. Weird, but great. But why haven't you gotten a pet for yourself before now?"

"I was afraid I would show favoritism, but I spoiled Cookie rotten despite my good intentions, and I adore him, and now he's mine, and I'm so excited I can hardly stand it. I've got to go tell him."

Hunter laughed, then ducked out of the way as Brenna dashed through the door. He hurried after her, realizing that he didn't want to miss any of the excitement. The fact that he, Hunter Emerson, Mr.

Practical and Logical of the Year, was caught up in the gaiety of a young woman gaining ownership of her favorite dog was absurd, to say the least. But Brenna's enthusiasm was infectious and, besides, he liked Cookie. It was nice that the furry mutt was a permanent member of the family. Well, Brenna's family. The whole thing actually had nothing to do with him.

Great, Hunter thought, as he went into the backyard. Now there was a dog to add to the husband and baby he'd envisioned in his scenario for Brenna. She was driving him nuts, turning his mind into scrambled eggs. He had no intention of making a commitment to her, yet the thought of another man touching her filled him with cold fury. His mood swings were becoming extreme, from a sense of euphoria when he was with Brenna, to bleak depression when he realized he really had no room for her in his life.

He watched Brenna open the gate to Cookie's runway, then drop to her knees and fling her arms around the dog's neck. A strange tightening in his throat caused Hunter to swallow heavily. Brenna found such joy in simple things, he mused. That was a gift for living life to the fullest that few people had. She found her happiness within each moment she was living, and asked so little of the future. It must have been how she had survived her unsettled childhood with the MacPhee.

Did she equate him with the MacPhee? he wondered. He hated the idea of being put into the same slot as her father, with what Hunter viewed as the selfish satisfying of the man's whims. Hunter's dream was not whimsical, it was real, concrete. Dammit, he wasn't like the MacPhee!

"Oh, Hunter," Brenna said, walking over to him, "do you think Cookie looks happy?"

"Sure he does," he said, smiling gently at her. "Cookie is a smart guy. He knows he's a lucky devil to be loved by you, Brenna. I don't know if dogs can feel love, but I know he'll be loyal to you, put you first, before anyone else. You deserve that, and I'm really glad it worked out that you can keep him."

"Thank you. I guess I'm being silly about a dog, but . . ."

"Not at all," he said, placing his hand on her cheek. "I just wish . . . Well, I don't know quite how to say this. If the timing were different, if my company didn't need so much of my attention . . . Brenna, I care for you very much. I feel like a real louse standing here realizing that a dog is going to be a better friend to you than I am. Cookie won't let you down, he'll always be there for you. He isn't going to make you cry."

Brenna frowned slightly as she gazed up at Hunter. She saw the flicker of pain in his eyes and heard the sadness in his voice. She lifted her hand and covered his where it rested on her cheek, so warm against her soft skin.

She didn't know what to say because everything Hunter said was true. If they *had* met at a later time, things might be so very different for them. But would time really bring about a lessening in Hunter's devotion to his work? The MacPhee had never tired of his quest for rainbows. With what measuring stick would Hunter decide that his company was big enough, his reputation solid, his name evoking enough respect and recognition in Portland? No, he might never change, and she had to accept that.

"Oh, Hunter," she said, sighing, "don't blame yourself for who you are, your attitudes, beliefs, your determination to succeed. If I've made you feel guilty somehow, that wasn't my intention."

"But you deserve—"

"No," she interrupted, "don't start all that again. I could say the same things, you know. I could tell you that you deserve a father who is proud of his son's accomplishments instead of his condemning you for listening to your drummer. Making long lists of how everything should be isn't going to bring about miraculous changes. Your father is standing in judgment of you, and that isn't right or fair. But you're standing in judgment of yourself in relation to me, and that's wrong too. I love you, Hunter, just the way you are."

With a throaty groan, he pulled her roughly into his arms. He held her tightly, burying his face in the fragrant cloud of her hair.

His precious, precious Brenna, he thought. Why wasn't he stronger, a better man, with the decency to walk out of her life and give her the chance to love someone who would give her what she deserved to have? How could he have lived for nearly thirty years and not known of his own selfishness? What kind of person was he to take so much from Brenna and give so little in return? But he couldn't leave her. Not now. Not yet. He couldn't leave his Brenna.

"I think a car just pulled in," he said quietly.

"Oh, it must be Clancey."

"You go ahead. I'll be along in a minute."

"Hunter . . ."

"You mustn't keep your new guest waiting," he said, forcing a smile.

She looked at him for a long moment, then nodded and hurried into the house.

With a sigh, Hunter sank onto the picnic bench. Cookie bounded over and rested his head on Hunter's knee. The dog's tail was wagging exuberantly and increased its tempo when Hunter scratched Cookie behind the ears.

"Well, ol' buddy," Hunter said, "you've had quite a birthday. You've just received the best present in the world: Brenna MacPhee. You're her very first pet, so you've got a big responsibility. Of course, I'm her first love and I'm blowing it straight to hell."

Cookie barked.

"Yeah, I figured you'd agree with me. Man, I'm really losing it. I'm sitting here carrying on a conversation with a dog!"

With a snort of disgust, Hunter stood up and walked across the yard. He entered the kitchen with Cookie right behind him.

"Good-bye," Brenna was saying in the living room. "Don't worry about a thing. I'll take very good care of Clancey."

The door closed, then the air reverberated with the strangest noise Hunter had ever heard. He hurried into the front room.

"Brenna, what—" he started, then stopped in his tracks.

Brenna was staring wide-eyed at an enormous basset hound who was sitting in the middle of the floor, his head thrown back, as he howled at the top of his lungs.

"Can you believe that?" Brenna said. "How can one dog make so much noise? Clancey, calm down.

Your parents will come back for you, I promise. Clancey?"

Cookie scrambled up the stairs and disappeared.

"Clancey!" Hunter boomed. "We are men here, not boys. Now, knock it off! Where's your pride? Your dignity? Clancey, zip your lip!"

Clancey clamped his mouth shut, stared at Hunter with big sad eyes, then sank into a dejected heap.

"My goodness," Brenna said, laughing, "that was wonderful, Hunter. How did you know what to say to him?"

"I saw that bit in a movie about new recruits going to Marine boot camp," Hunter said, appearing very pleased with himself. "I swear, Brenna, that is the ugliest dog I've ever seen."

"Oh, I don't know, he's got some endearing qualities, I'm sure. It's not his fault he's saggy and wrinkled. He looks so sad, though."

"Not necessarily. He could be happy as a clam, and he'd probably still look like that. There, see? He wagged his tail. Everything is fine."

"Thanks to you," she said, smiling at Hunter. "If he starts howling again, I'll try sounding like a drill sergeant."

"You can always call me, and I'll yell at him over the phone. Seriously, Brenna, if Clancey goes nuts, I'll come over and help you. You've got your hands full with all your guests. I mean it. If you need me, I'll be here in a flash."

"I couldn't ask you to do that."

"Yes! You don't have to tackle everything alone anymore. I'm here, I'm part of your life. I know I'm not everything I should be for you, but I sure as hell wouldn't let you down in an emergency. Will you promise to call if you need me?"

"Well, I don't know."

"Brenna!"

"Yes, all right," she said, throwing up her hands. "You're doing your Marine bit again."

"Don't feel you have to salute," he said, grinning. "A simple 'Yes, sir' will do."

"You're pushing it, Emerson."

"Just do as you're told, MacPhee," he said. He gathered her into his arms and kissed her thoroughly.

Apparently, Clancey did not approve of losing his position as the center of attention, and cut loose with an ear-splitting howl.

Neither Brenna nor Hunter noticed.

Seven

If Charlotte Emerson was surprised that her son suddenly appeared in her living room at noon on Monday, she hid it very well. If she was amazed that he was dressed in gray slacks and a bright red V-neck sweater worn over a shirt and tie, she made no comment. She simply kissed him on the cheek, waved him onto the sofa, then sat down on a chair while waiting for him to speak.

"Well!" Hunter said, a trifle loudly. "How's life treating you, Mother?"

"Fine," she said, suppressing a smile. "Would you like some lunch?"

"No, thanks, I've eaten. I think. Yeah, Maggie brought some sandwiches in. She does that, you know, makes sure I eat. Great gal, that Maggie. Salt of the earth. I'm babbling, right?"

"Yes, dear, I'd definitely say that you are. Why don't you tell me what's bothering you about Brenna?"

Hunter opened his mouth, clamped it shut again, then frowned. "How did you know that I need to talk about Brenna?"

"I'm your mother and I love you. I saw the way you were looking at her when you two were here. I could tell that there is something wonderful happening between you. She's a lovely woman, Hunter, and obviously very different from the other women you've dated."

"Yes, she is. I've never known anyone like Brenna. Got three hours? I'll tell you all the reasons she's so special." He smiled. "And thanks for not mentioning that her dress was the same material as the guest room curtains."

Charlotte laughed. "It was a darling dress. That material looked much nicer on Brenna than it does on our boring old windows. So, Hunter? You've met a delightful young woman, who obviously has you in a dither. Why is that distressing you?"

"Because I can't give her the time and attention that she needs. I have my company to think of, Mother. It has to be my first priority. Your son, the louse, should leave Brenna MacPhee alone so she can find the right man for her. But have I walked out of her life? Hell, no. I see her every free minute I have, fit her in when I have time. Lord, that stinks."

"And Brenna?" Charlotte asked. "What is she saying about all of this?"

"She . . . she's in love with me. She says she understands that I have to listen for my drummer."

"Pardon me?"

"My inner voice. She knows how important my business is, and has no intention of asking more of me than I can give. But she deserves more, don't you see? She has a father who always placed her second, and now a lover who— What I mean is—"

"A lover who is placing her second too," Charlotte said, nodding. "The word 'lover' doesn't shock me, dear. I do know about the birds and the bees." Her gaze flickered over Hunter's red sweater. "You don't see yourself changing in the future?"

"No, I can't! I have too much work to do. I have a reputation to establish in Portland."

"Ahh, yes, the establishing of *your* name. Hunter, are you in love with Brenna?"

"No. I care very deeply for her, but I have no intention of falling in love with her."

"My dear boy, you can't control your emotions like you do your computers. There's no button to push to turn love off when it happens to you. You're intelligent enough to know that."

"I'm intelligent enough to control my own destiny. There is no room for love in my immediate future. Everything would be fine if I didn't feel so damn guilty about staying close to Brenna when I know I should leave her alone. That's really ripping me up. I can't . . . Well, I just can't seem to stay away from her."

"Do tell," Charlotte said under her breath, as she hid another smile.

"What?"

"Nothing. I think you're creating problems where there aren't any. After all, you did say that Brenna understands your need to devote yourself to your work. It doesn't sound to me like she'd want you to feel guilty about it."

"No, she doesn't. She's very adamant about that, but second place is all she's ever known. I hate the thought of being like the MacPhee."

"Who?"

"Her father, the MacPhee. Oh, man, I'm in a helluva mess here."

"No, I don't think so. You're just used to having everything under control by the application of logic and analysis. That's fine for numbers, dear, but you have to make allowances when dealing with people. Just relax and take one day at a time for now. Quit being so hard on yourself."

"Mrs. Emerson," Annie said from the doorway, "I don't mean to interrupt, but you did say you had that committee meeting this afternoon."

"Oh, yes, I must be on my way," Charlotte said, getting to her feet. Hunter stood also. "We'll talk again if you like, dear," Charlotte said. "You know I'm always here if you need me."

"Thank you, Mother."

"How is it you had time to come by in the middle of the day?"

"Well, I was supposed to get a haircut, but I've decided to let my hair grow a bit. No sense in going around looking like I'm in the military."

She laughed. "Oh, I see."

"Hair is funny?" he asked.

"No. No, of course not. I must dash." She kissed him on the cheek. "Enjoy each new day, Hunter. I think that's the best way to handle this situation with Brenna for now. Good-bye, dear."

"Bye," he said.

After his mother had left Hunter walked slowly from the room and headed toward the front door. On impulse he turned and strode down the long hall, through the kitchen, and out into the backyard. The perfectly manicured lawn was a plush carpet beneath his feet as he strolled to a white latticework gazebo.

As he entered the charming enclosure and sank onto the wooden bench, memories of his childhood rushed over him. He recalled the hours spent in the gazebo studying, daydreaming, talking with his buddies. It had been his private domain and his sisters had learned very quickly not to intrude. He had solved the endless problems of his adolescence by sifting through the facts and reaching a conclusion in the solitude of the gazebo. It had been here that he had realized he could never be a lawyer to please his father. Big decisions and small had been made in this special place.

He rested his elbows on his knees and made a steeple of his fingers as he allowed the tranquility of the setting to seep into him. He felt his tense muscles relax and drew a deep breath. But then it was there again, that unknown entity within him.

"Damn," he muttered, and stood up and began to pace.

The sun ducked behind a cloud and shadows fell over the gazebo as Hunter continued to pace, lost in thought. Then suddenly the sun burst free, sending a bright beacon of light over the enclosure and leaving the remainder of the yard in an eerie semidarkness.

Hunter stopped and glanced around as he found himself bathed in the sunlight. He registered a feeling of panic, then dismissed it as ridiculous. Then slowly, slowly, the mysterious force within him became clear, shouting its name, revealing its identity.

Love.

He was in love with Brenna MacPhee!

"Lord, no!" he said, sinking onto the bench. "No!"

But his heart, soul, and mind whispered yes, over and over, louder and louder. It beat against his brain and caused an ache in his temples.

"Dammit to hell," he said fiercely. "Now what am I going to do?"

The day had been long and exhausting for Brenna. She had bathed each of the dogs in a metal tub in the backyard, and her muscles ached from restraining the animals, who had had no desire to have a bubble bath. Clancey had howled his way through his turn, and Cookie had hidden under her bed after being towel-dried.

She had showered and shampooed her hair, then collapsed on the bed in her robe, deciding she wouldn't move for a week. Her hand had slid over to the side of the bed where Hunter had spent the night, and a soft smile had formed on her lips.

Such sweet, sensuous lovemaking they had shared, she mused dreamily. And what bliss it had been to wake in the morning snuggled close to Hunter's warm, naked body. In a bold moment that had surprised her, she had kissed him awake, then trailed her hands over his body until he was moaning with pleasure. Their joining at dawn had been rough and urgent. It had been ecstasy.

Suddenly she recalled a legend she'd heard when she and the MacPhee had been living in Kentucky. A man's wife, an old woman had told Brenna, sleeps on his right. His mistress, when he snuck off to see her, was delegated to sleep on his left.

"I slept on the wife's side," Brenna said, popping

straight up. "I did! Oh, how silly." She flopped back against the pillows. But, oh, how glorious it would be to be Hunter's wife, have his child, spend the rest of her life with the man she loved.

Stop it, Brenna, she told herself, slipping off the bed. Quit daydreaming. Hunter had never said he loved her, let alone had any thoughts for the future. His company came first. But, darn it, she loved that man. And she had a chilling fear that when all was said and done, she'd be left alone to cry.

With a wobbly sigh, she opened her closet and reached for clean clothes. She'd wear a dress, she decided, to perk up her mood. The animals had been fed their dinner, and she would dine in style. Would Hunter come over? She didn't know, as he hadn't mentioned it when he'd left that morning. All she could do was wait and see if he showed up. That was how it would always be, she supposed, but tonight it seemed very hard to accept.

"Shame on you, Brenna MacPhee," she said. "You know the facts, so quit whining."

The dress was a pale-blue gauzy cotton that had a puckered appearance, as though it needed ironing, but was actually supposed to look that way. A thin gold thread weaved through the material, and the neckline was scooped to just above her breasts.

"Terrific, kiddo," she said to her reflection in the mirror. "You're a real knockout." If Hunter didn't come by, it would be his loss, she told herself. Oh, ha! If she spent the evening alone, she'd be miserable, and she knew it. How could being in love be so wonderful and so depleting at the same time?

Cookie poked his head out from beneath the bed and apparently decided to forgive Brenna for the indignity of his bath. He wiggled out to greet her, then followed close behind as she skipped down the stairs. Just as she reached the bottom, the buzzer sounded at the front door, and she hurried to answer it.

"Hunter," she said, an instant smile on her face. "Come in. What a yummy sweater. You look terrific in red."

"What? Oh, thanks. You're all dressed up. Were you planning on going out?"

"No, I just decided to get gussied up for a change."

"Well, you're lovely, very beautiful," he said, then wandered across the room to stare at the old player piano.

Brenna closed the door and frowned. Something was wrong, she thought. Hunter was edgy. She could virtually feel the tension emanating from him. He hadn't smiled. He hadn't touched or kissed her. Dear heaven, what was the matter?

"Does this piano work?" he asked, glancing at her over his shoulder.

"I only have one roller for it," she said, walking to his side. "It's a rather tinny version of a waltz I've never heard before."

"Why don't you turn it on?"

Why don't you kiss me? "All right," she said, pressing a lever.

The piano creaked, groaned, then the keys began to move up and down as the music began.

"May I have this dance, Miss MacPhee?" Hunter asked quietly.

"I'd be honored, Mr. Emerson."

He held her away from him as he guided her across the floor in time to the old-fashioned waltz.

She inhaled his heady aftershave, and felt the heat from his hand where it rested on her back. Her fingers caressed the soft material of his sweater, and felt the steely muscles beneath. She wanted to move closer, mold herself to his body, press her lips to his. She wanted him to tell her that everything was fine, that it was only her imagination that something was wrong. His tension seemed to weave its way inside her, though, causing her to stiffen in his arms. The music played on, but she hardly heard it over the rushing noise in her ears.

Hunter clenched his jaw and spun Brenna around in time to the music. He could feel the change in her, the wariness. She knew something was wrong with him. It had taken every ounce of his self-control not to pull her into his arms and kiss her when he'd walked into the room. She was a vision of loveliness in that dress. She was Brenna. He loved her.

And he'd come to say good-bye.

He was going to walk away from the only woman he had ever loved. He had to, before all his dreams and goals were smothered under the heavy weight of love. It was the only logical, practical thing to do, and it hurt like hell. He couldn't have Brenna and still accomplish what he had set out to do with his company. Hunter Emerson Consulting Corporation had to come first. And now that he knew that he was in love with Brenna, he couldn't have her at all.

Hunter was filled with the greatest pain he had ever known.

The music stopped, and he stepped back quickly, glancing over at the piano. "That was nice," he said. "Thank you."

"Hunter?" Brenna said, placing her hand on his arm. "What's wrong? Please, Hunter, tell me."

He slowly turned his head to look at her, and her breath caught in her throat when she saw the haunting pain in his eyes. Her heart beat wildly as she searched his face for an answer, fearing what she might find. Silence hung in the room like an oppressive weight, and she could hardly breathe.

"Hunter?" she whispered.

"Brenna, I . . ." he began, then cleared his throat roughly. "I— The buzzer. There's someone at the door."

"I don't care. Talk to me. Please!"

The buzzer sounded again, and Hunter swore under his breath as he strode to the door and flung it open.

"Howdy!" a large man boomed.

"MacPhee!" Brenna cried. "Oh, MacPhee!"

The MacPhee entered the room and Brenna flung herself into his arms. He spun her around, his laughter bouncing off the walls.

Hunter frowned as he closed the door and watched the scene before him. The MacPhee was enormous, at least six feet four, with a barrel chest and wide shoulders. His hair was brown and fell well past the collar of his red-and-black plaid flannel shirt. He sported a full beard and moustache. Brenna looked like a tiny doll as she clung to her father's neck.

"Ahh, my darlin' Brenna," the MacPhee said, setting her on her feet. "You look like an angel, pretty as a picture."

"Oh, MacPhee," she said, grasping his hands, "it's so wonderful to see you. You promised to be here for Christmas this year. Does this mean you'll be staying until then?"

"Well, now," the MacPhee said, turning to Hunter, "who might you be, boy?"

"Hunter Emerson," he said, extending his hand. The MacPhee shook it with such exuberance, Hunter was sure he'd be crippled for life. "I've heard a lot about you, sir," he said. And none of it good, he mentally tacked on.

" 'Tis a fact?" the MacPhee said, grinning. "My baby girl's been talking about her MacPhee, has she? And you? What are you to my Brenna, Hunter?"

"MacPhee," Brenna said quickly, "there will be plenty of time for you and Hunter to get acquainted. Have you had dinner? I haven't, so we can eat together. Where's your suitcase? You *are* staying until Christmas, aren't you? You promised we'd be together, have a tree and everything."

"I know I said that, Brenna," he said, "but, well, my plans have been changed a bit."

"A bit?" she repeated. "How much is a bit? MacPhee, where is your suitcase?"

"It's on the steamer. We just pulled in here to refuel. Now, isn't this a lucky break, I said to myself. I'll get to see my Brenna, and here I am."

"And Christmas?" she asked quietly. "What about Christmas, MacPhee?"

"Darlin' girl, I'll be somewhere in Alaska. But next year, yes, next year, I promise I'll be home for the holidays."

Damn him! Hunter thought, seeing the stricken expression on Brenna's face. Damn that selfish, sorry son of a gun. And he called himself a father? Hell.

"But lookee here, my girl," the MacPhee said. "I brought you another unicorn." He reached in his pocket and pulled out the tiny figurine. "Real jade, this one is," he said, placing it in Brenna's hand and curling her fingers around it. "You look at that on Christmas morning and know I'll be thinking of you."

"Yes, of course," Brenna whispered.

"It's off with me now," he said, hugging Brenna tightly. "Take care of my girl, Hunter," he added, whopping him on the shoulder.

"Yeah, right," Hunter said, definitely not smiling.

"Good-bye, MacPhee," Brenna said, as the door closed behind him. "Merry Christmas," she added, a sob catching in her throat. She uncurled her fingers and stared at the unicorn, tears streaming down her cheeks.

"Oh, Brenna," Hunter said, closing the distance between them and pulling her into his arms. "I'm so sorry this happened. What can I say? How can I help you? Brenna, please don't cry."

"No, no, I'm not," she said, stepping back and brushing the tears from her cheeks. "I'm not crying. I'm fine. The MacPhee just took me by surprise, that's all. I thought maybe, just maybe, he'd keep his promise this year and be with me at Christmas, but—" Her tears started again. "But he remembered my unicorn so I really shouldn't feel bad."

"Yes, dammit, you should!" Hunter said. "I can't believe that man. He has no idea of how much he's hurt you."

"He has to listen for—"

"No! His drummer didn't tell him to stroll in here

and break his daughter's heart. The MacPhee did that on his own. He's selfish and self-centered and—"

"Stop it!" she yelled. "You're talking about my father. I've accepted the MacPhee the way he is, and I love him. You have no right to stand there and pass judgment on him. I'm going to go put my unicorn on the shelf." She ran across the room and up the stairs.

"Damn," Hunter said, raking his hand through his hair. He walked to the bottom of the stairs and stared up. With slow steps he went in search of Brenna.

Brenna entered her living room and hurried to the shelf on the wall. With a shaking hand she placed the jade unicorn next to the others, then looked at the collection, tears again filling her eyes.

Why, MacPhee? She asked silently. Why had he broken his promise again? One day. Christmas Day. That was all she had asked for, hoped for, dreamed about. They would have decorated a little tree and listened to carols on the radio; strung popcorn on thread while a delicious turkey baked in the oven. Gaily wrapped packages would have been beneath the tree and— No, she had to stop this. She was acting foolish.

Hunter came up behind her and placed his hands on her shoulders.

"Come away from the unicorns," he said gently. "Looking at them will only make you more unhappy."

She leaned back against him, feeling his strength. Dear heaven, she thought, she was suddenly so tired. It was as though the last ounce of energy had been drained from her body.

"They're very nice unicorns," she said, her voice trembling. "I'm really very fortunate to have a father who gives me such lovely gifts."

"Ah, babe, don't," Hunter said, turning her to face him. "Listen to me, Brenna. I know you love the MacPhee, but you've got to start protecting yourself against the hurt he causes you. You allowed yourself to believe he'd keep his promise when he's broken it so many times before. Don't let him do this to you. Love him, but don't trust him."

"I'm not sure I can do that, Hunter. I have to believe in the people I love. You know that I love you. Would you want me to hold a portion of myself back, build a wall between us to protect myself from you?"

"We're not talking about me," he said. Not now! his mind screamed. How could he face the fact that he had come here tonight to hurt her, and the MacPhee had beaten him to it? Hunter's goals were legitimate, his reasons for leaving Brenna real and logical. The MacPhee's were pipe dreams. But Hunter knew the soundness of his having to go wouldn't lessen Brenna's pain. He couldn't tell her, not tonight. "You should eat," he said. "Would you like to go out to dinner?"

"No, thank you. I'm really not hungry. I'm acting very childish about having the MacPhee here at Christmas. It's a holiday that's centered on children, and I'm an adult. I can see why you prefer facts and logical data. Fantasies have a tendency to not come true. It's not the MacPhee's fault, it's mine, for placing too much importance on a single day of the year."

"A man has to be responsible for his actions," Hunter said. "Promises are made to be kept, or at least every possible effort made to keep them. Don't excuse the MacPhee so easily. I'm not saying you should stop loving him, but see him for what he is."

"Love him, but not like him? The way you feel about your father?"

"Something like that, I guess."

She frowned, then moved out of Hunter's embrace and sank onto the sofa with a weary sigh. Cookie wandered through the open door and curled up at her feet.

"Hunter," she said, looking over at him, "do you think your attitude toward your father protects you against being hurt by his disapproval of your career?"

"Yes, I do. I just don't allow his remarks to get to me anymore."

"Then why . . ." She hesitated, then took a deep breath. "Then why are you determined to make a name for your company in Portland? *Your* name, Hunter. Why, if it's not to gain your father's approval after all?"

Hunter frowned and his jaw tightened. "That's crazy," he said.

"Is it? Are we really so different, Hunter? I want the MacPhee's actions to prove that he loves me, that he's willing to put me first in his life, just once. That's all, just once. I would have had that proof if he'd kept his promise about Christmas. But he didn't. And you? You've done wonderful things with your company, but your father still won't acknowledge your efforts. So you push for more. The Hunter Emerson Consulting Corporation has to be the best, so that your father will see you as a successful man and be proud, rather than viewing you as a disobedient little boy."

"You don't know what you're talking about, Brenna!" Hunter snapped.

"Don't I?" she asked softly. "I think perhaps I do."

"Why do we keep shifting this around to me?" Hunter said, frowning. "I'm not the one who just got blown away by my father, you are. All I'm trying to do is prevent it from happening again. The MacPhee sure as hell isn't going to change, so *you'll* have to. The man just doesn't give a damn, Brenna. You'd better accept that." Oh, hell, he thought, what was he doing? He had no right to rip into Brenna like that. She'd pushed him about his father, and now he was lashing back. She was totally wrong about why he wanted his company to prosper, but that didn't mean he had to get vicious and cruel. "I'm sorry," he said. "I shouldn't have said that. I'm sure the MacPhee loves you, Brenna."

"Yes, he does, in his own way. I really don't want to discuss this anymore. I brought on my own sorrow by expecting more of the MacPhee than he's able to give. End of story. We need to back up to where you were going to tell me what was bothering you when you were acting so strangely earlier."

"It was nothing," he said, sinking onto the sofa next to her.

"It was, and you know it. Please, Hunter, we're based on honesty, remember? What were you about to tell me when my father arrived?"

He picked up her hand and laced his fingers through hers. "I have to go out of town for a couple of days, that's all," he said, staring at their entwined hands. "I'm going down to L.A. to bid on a job for a restaurant project. I . . . um, just hated the thought of leaving you."

"You're sure that's all it was?"

"Positive," he said, shifting to face her. "I really think you should eat some dinner."

"No." She shook her head. "Are you hungry? I could fix you something."

"No, I'm not hungry at all. Oh, Brenna, you look so worn out and pale. Would you like me to leave so you can get some rest?"

Leave? she thought, startled. Leave her all alone? Oh, not tonight. She didn't want to be alone tonight. She felt as though her world was suddenly topsy-turvy, with everything out of place. She would have the task of setting things to rights again. She'd have to push the heartache of the MacPhee's broken promise from her mind, forgive and forget that he had placed her second yet again. And she still couldn't rid herself of the suspicion that something was wrong with Hunter. Something more than just his having to go out of town. But she was too tired to deal with it all tonight, and she didn't want to be alone.

"Brenna?"

"Would you stay?" she asked, looking directly into his eyes.

"If that's what you want."

"I'd rather not be alone. I've been alone for a long time, but tonight I just don't think I could handle it."

"I understand, I really do. You're emotionally drained, and that can be more depleting than physical labor."

"And I gave all the dogs baths," she said, then sniffled. "And Clancey howled, and Cookie was so mad at me he hid under the bed and— Oh, darn!" she said, and burst into tears.

"Hey, come here," Hunter said, smiling as he gathered her close to him. "What you need is some old-fashioned pampering. I swear, even your curls look tired. You go crawl in bed and I'll bring you a tray of food."

"Oh, no, you don't have to do that."

"I want to. You can pretend that you're in a fancy hotel and ordered room service."

"I have to put the dogs in their runways once more tonight."

"I can handle that. No problem."

"You're a very nice person, Hunter Emerson," she said, smiling at him through her tears.

"Yeah, I'm a real gem," he said. Right up there on the list with the MacPhee. "*You* are in bed. *I'm* in the kitchen. Go!"

"Thank you," she said, then pressed her lips to his.

No! his mind raged. He didn't have the right to kiss her, make love to her, or even hold her in his arms. He was going to hurt her, make her cry—just like the MacPhee had. That crumb had at least given her a unicorn, but Hunter would give nothing. He couldn't take from her, not again.

"Kiss me, Hunter," she whispered, her lips against his. "I want you to kiss me."

"It won't stop there, and you know it," he said hoarsely, straining to control his own desire. "You're tired and—"

"Oh, Hunter, please don't say no to me. I feel so strange, like I've splintered into a million pieces and I don't have the energy to put myself back together. I don't want to think, I just want to feel. Feel you, inside me. When we make love, we're one. One, Hunter. There's no first or second place. We're equal, together, sharing everything that is happening to us. Please," she finished, nearly choking on a sob.

"Oh, damn," he muttered, then brought his mouth down hard onto hers.

He hated himself. And he couldn't stop himself.

Hunter's tongue delved deep into Brenna's mouth, and she moaned with pleasure as she circled his neck with her arms to urge him closer. Her breasts were crushed against his chest as his hands roamed over her back. The blood pounded in his veins and his manhood was hot, aching with the need for Brenna MacPhee. His mind screamed in disapproval, but Hunter ignored the voice of his conscience. The knife of guilt twisted in his gut, but he paid no attention to the pain.

Brenna wanted him. And he loved her.

They would have tonight, he told himself. He would erase from her heart the hurt of the MacPhee's betrayal. They would be one, just as she had said. But she *would* be placed first in their union, her pleasure assured before his own. He would give her the strength of his body because he could not give her the commitment of his soul. But it was a second-place gift, just like the unicorn.

"Hunter, love me," she said. "Now. I want you now."

He lifted her into his arms and carried her into the bedroom. His throat constricted with emotion as he saw the love, desire, and trust reflected in her dark eyes. With trembling hands he removed her clothing, then his own. He laid her on the bed and stretched out next to her. No words were spoken as he kissed and caressed every inch of her silken body. His muscles ached from the tension of his restraint, but still he held back, teasing, tasting, bringing her to a fever pitch of desire.

"Hunter!" she cried.

He entered her slowly, sensuously, heightening her passion until she sobbed with the need for him. Then at last, *at last*, he moved fully into her honeyed warmth, lifting her away, taking her to the place she so desperately sought.

Hunter felt as though he were being hurled into space as he reached the summit of his own climb to ecstasy. His body shuddered over and over, and a rushing noise filled his ears.

He heard a raspy voice speaking into the darkness, hardly recognizing it as his own.

"I love you, Brenna," he gasped. "Dear God, how I love you!"

Eight

Brenna woke and blinked several times in the darkness, not knowing what had brought her from her cocoon of dreamless sleep. She was nestled close to Hunter, her hand resting on his chest where she could feel the steady beat of his heart.

Then she knew why she was awake. Cookie was snoring. She smiled and slid off the bed, then walked to where Cookie was curled up on the floor. She poked him gently, he shifted position, and the noise stopped. Back in bed, she shivered and snuggled next to Hunter, relishing the heat emanating from his body.

Hunter, she thought. He had said that he loved her.

She sifted the words through her heart and soul, savoring them, allowing them to fill her with infinite joy. She tucked the precious gift in a special place in her mind, then frowned.

She was playing games, fantasizing, and she

knew it. Hunter had declared his love in a moment of passion raging out of control. And he'd never said the words again.

After their lovemaking, they had lain quietly. Finally, Hunter had dressed and told her he would tend to the dogs, then return with a tray of food fit for a queen. He had been cheerful and chatty, rambling on about various topics as he'd propped a tray containing eggs, toast, tea, and fruit across her lap. She had laughed in all the right places, expressed her thanks for the delectable meal, and willed herself not to cry. She had seen through his charade. The tension radiating from Hunter had hung heavily in the air.

What should she do? she asked herself now. Press him for an answer? Tell him she knew there was more wrong than just his having to leave town? Demand to know what was the matter? Did she really want to know? In the aftermath of the MacPhee's broken promise, did she really want to hear what Hunter had to say?

No, she realized, she didn't. Not now. Not yet. She was too fragile, she needed time to regain her emotional strength after the blow the MacPhee had dealt her. So she would wait. She'd pretend that everything was fine, live in a potentially dangerous fantasy world for a while, and face the truth later. She might even throw caution to the wind and repeat again and again Hunter's treasured words, I love you.

How foolishly she was behaving, she thought. There were warning signs everywhere telling her that things were not what they should be, and she was ignoring them, burying her head like an ostrich. But she didn't care. It would all catch up with her, she knew it, but for now she didn't care.

She closed her eyes and slept, but it wasn't the peaceful sleep she was accustomed to. Instead, she was haunted by a dream that caused her to toss and turn, trying to escape from the frightening scene.

The MacPhee was there, but he was dressed in dark slacks and a white shirt, his beard gone, his hair neatly trimmed. Hunter was next to him in the MacPhee's flannel shirt with a sable-colored beard covering half of his face. The two men were laughing and talking, while Brenna stood behind a glass partition shouting at them to acknowledge that she was there. They seemed oblivious to her presence as she screamed their names, begging them to hear her, free her from her prison.

Then arm and arm, Hunter and the MacPhee strode forward to break a ribbon that had suddenly materialized. A unicorn pranced toward them and presented each with a foot-high first-place trophy. The unicorn then came to the glass enclosure and shook its head sadly before sticking a small seal on the window. It read, "Second Place, Forever."

"No!" Brenna said, sitting bolt upright in the bed. "No!"

She turned her head quickly, but Hunter was gone. Her heart raced as she snatched up the note propped on the nightstand.

"Brenna," it read, "I'll see you when I get back from L.A. Hunter."

"Oh?" she said aloud. "Not, 'Love, Hunter'? What a nice impersonal message." How bitter she sounded, she realized, and fed up, and ticked off, and plain old mad as hell!

She jumped off the bed, pulled on her robe, and began to pace the floor with thudding steps. Her lips were pursed together, her eyes narrowed, and her curls bounced about her head in wild disarray. One thought repeated itself over and over in her mind.

She was sick to death of being second!

It was time, by gum, for Brenna MacPhee to be first!

No, she thought, stopping her flight to tap her finger against her chin, she wouldn't attempt to change the MacPhee. But Hunter Emerson? That was a different story. Hunter's tunnel vision about his company, his driving need to establish his name in Portland, was due to his father's attitude, she was sure of it. Frank Emerson was pushing Hunter's buttons, and Hunter didn't even realize it. She was also convinced that Hunter loved her. Darn it, he did!

Well, the old Brenna, Miss Second Place of the Century, would have settled for whatever emotional crumbs Hunter tossed her way. But no more. No, sir, she was going to be a winner, come in first. Mr. Logical and Practical Emerson had better gear up, because she was prepared to do battle. She loved that man, and was not going to give him up without a fight.

"I have spoken," she said, poking a finger in the air. "Victory shall be mine."

Brenna was busy the remainder of the day. She performed the ongoing chores at the Pet Palace, then telephoned Cindy and asked her to babysit. Cindy said she would be there after her last class, which ended at four.

"Got a date with Hunter the Hunk?" she had asked.

"Nope," Brenna had said. "A rendezvous with a shopping mall."

"That's almost as good."

It was close to nine-thirty when Brenna returned home, her arms laden with bags and boxes.

"My goodness," Cindy said, "did you inherit a bunch of money?"

"No, I simply decided it was time for some new clothes," Brenna said, setting her purchases on the sofa. "I deserve it, because I'm an extremely nice person."

"Indeed you are. So, do I get a fashion show? This is exciting!"

"I'm too exhausted to try it all on again," Brenna said, sinking onto the sofa and kicking off her shoes. "Do look at what I bought, though. I'm eager to see your reactions."

Brenna beamed in delight at Cindy's ooh's and aah's, then whooped with laughter when Cindy shrieked, "Are you sure this is legal?"

"Who cares?" Brenna said breezily.

"Hunter is going to die, absolutely die," Cindy said. "I've never seen such gorgeous, sexy, slinky, yummy stuff. You sure went first class."

"First place, Cindy," Brenna said. "The goal here is first place."

Cindy left a short time later still chattering about how she wished she could be a mouse in the corner when Hunter got a glimpse of Brenna in her new wardrobe.

Brenna completed the last round of evening chores, showered, then crawled into bed. Cookie was asleep on the floor. Snoring.

That night Brenna MacPhee slept like a baby.

Hunter Emerson did not.

In his hotel room in Los Angeles, Hunter lay in bed, staring up into the darkness. He was not smiling.

Had he told Brenna that he loved her? The question repeated itself over and over in his mind. Lord knew that he'd been thinking it while he'd made love to her, but had he opened his mouth and said it? No, no, he couldn't have, or Brenna surely would have responded in some way. So, okay, his body had been out of control, but he'd maintained command of his mind and his big mouth.

Hadn't he?

No, he hadn't said it, Hunter decided firmly. Brenna had been calm and cheerful when he'd brought her the tray of food, then had fallen asleep in his arms. She'd given no indication that she had just been told that he was in love with her. At least she'd seemed calm, but he had been so tense, how could he be certain? He was driving himself crazy. He'd just have to believe he hadn't verbally declared his love for Brenna MacPhee.

He thought again of her father. The selfish, uncaring, sleazeball MacPhee. Creating a child did not qualify a man to be a father. Now, when *he* became a father, Hunter thought, the child would have love and attention. Its mother, his wife, would be his best friend, the focal point of his life. His child would make his own career choice, and he would encourage his offspring to go for it, listen for his drummer, do his own thing. Hunter would do a damn good job when he married Brenna and—

"What?" he said aloud. "Who?" No, he wasn't

marrying Brenna MacPhee! Granted, he loved her. And, yes, she'd be beautiful as she carried their child. Of course she'd be a wonderful wife and mother. But Brenna was in the here and now. Any shadowy plans he might have regarding a family were in the distant future, and they didn't include Brenna. To stay with her now would defeat his purpose. His love would erode his energies, his time, and his determination to make the most of his company.

And that was another thing. Where did Brenna get off saying that he was pushing himself to succeed to gain his father's approval? Ridiculous. He couldn't care less what his father thought. But his father *would* come to see that he had done a helluva job of— No! It didn't matter what his father saw! Darn that Brenna! She was full of beans!

Enough, Hunter thought. He had to get organized, figure out the next step to take. Due to the MacPhee's broken promise, Brenna was fragile at the moment. He couldn't leave her until he was sure she had regained her mental equilibrium. He owed her that much, and besides, he loved her. He'd stick around until he knew she was all right. It wasn't particularly dangerous, since now that he knew he loved her, he was back in control of himself.

Was Brenna sleeping? he wondered. She wouldn't still be crying because of the MacPhee, would she? If he were there, Hunter thought, he'd hold her in his arms, kiss away her sorrow, make love to her if that was what she wanted. He'd felt guilty as sin about touching her last night, but she had wants and needs. Who was he to tell her they shouldn't make love?

He rolled over onto his stomach and punched his pillow. He'd finished the bid he'd come to L.A. to do. He usually took two days to calculate a bid that size, but he'd had a driving need to get it done. Nervous energy, he supposed, from the unsettling events with Brenna and the MacPhee. So he'd decided to stay over in L.A. and relax for the extra day. Lord, he needed to relax. He was wired, like a tight spring.

But Brenna was alone. And what if she was crying?

Maybe, he mused, he should just go on back to Portland and check on her. He could get an early flight, then casually drop by the Pet Palace and see if she was all right. It was the least he could do to help her get over the hurt caused by the MacPhee. Yeah, good idea. He'd take her some flowers. That would perk her up. This rushing back to Portland had nothing to do with his love for Brenna, he told himself. It was because she was in a bad place right now, and he was basically a nice guy. The love number was under control.

With a satisfied nod Hunter closed his eyes and drifted off to sleep, his arm spread across the empty expanse of bed next to him.

Brenna was dusting the furniture in the downstairs living room when the buzzer sounded. She opened the front door and her eyes widened in shock.

"Hunter," she said. "What are you doing here? I thought you were in Los Angeles."

"May I come in?" he asked, smiling at her.

"Oh, yes, of course," she said, stepping back for

him to enter. Sexy jeans again, she thought wildly. Those sexy, sexy jeans, and a black and gray striped sweater. Whew! Was it her imagination or was Hunter's hair a tad longer than it was before? Oh, how she adored that hair. Oh, dear, she had to pay attention when he was speaking to her. "Pardon me?" she said.

"The flowers. They're for you," he said, handing her a bouquet. Would she notice if he hauled her into his arms, kissed her senseless, then ripped her clothes from her body? he wondered. Knock it off, Emerson.

"Thank you," she said, throwing her arms around his neck. "No one has ever given me flowers before."

This was her decision, Hunter told himself. Hers.

The kiss was long and powerful. Their tongues met as their bodies molded together, and Brenna felt passion explode within her. Their hands roamed over each other until she didn't think she could stand it any longer. It was fantastic.

Hunter finally lifted his head and blinked once slowly to bring himself back to reality. Brenna leaned her head against his chest, inhaling his aroma, relishing his heat and strength.

"You'd better get those flowers into water," he said, moving her away from him. Slowly, reluctantly moving her away from him.

"Yes, of course," she said, her voice trembling slightly. "How did you manage to get back so soon?" she asked.

"Finished the job, that's all," he said, lifting one shoulder in a shrug as he followed her into the kitchen. "Hey, Cookie, how's my buddy?" he said when he saw the dog lying on the kitchen floor. Cookie wiggled in delight from head to toe.

"His snoring is getting worse every night," Brenna said, laughing. "I hope he doesn't have sinus problems. Oh, Hunter, these flowers are lovely," she added as she arranged them in a vase. "Thank you so much."

"My pleasure," he said. "How are you, Brenna? Doing okay?"

"In regard to what?" she asked, turning to look at him.

"The MacPhee."

"I'm fine."

"You are?" he asked, frowning. "No you're not."

"Yes I am, thanks to you. I know I was in terrible shape that night after the MacPhee left, but you were so kind and gentle, so wonderful. I've settled down about it now. I won't make the mistake of counting on the MacPhee's promises again. You made me realize that I must be realistic about my father. So, you see, I really am all right now, and I'm very grateful to you for your understanding."

"Oh," Hunter said, his frown deepening. "You're welcome. Glad I was here." Well, hell, now what? he asked himself. She was all glued back together about the MacPhee! Or . . . maybe she just thought she was. He'd better stick around a while yet and make sure. "Want to go out to dinner tonight?" he asked, smiling again.

"I'd love to."

"I'll pick you up at eight. No, make that seven. Well, I'd better get to the office."

"I didn't know you wore jeans to work."

"I don't have any appointments because I was supposed to be out of town. No sense in wearing good slacks when it isn't necessary. That's not very practical, because they have to go to the cleaners and it's time-consuming."

"Of course," she said, smiling. "I see you've decided to save time by not going to your barber too."

"Yeah, well, it got a little boring looking at the same hairstyle every morning in the mirror. I thought I'd grow it out a little."

"I really like it, Hunter."

"Oh?" He appeared rather pleased. "You do?"

She wove her fingers through the thick hair. "Oh, yes," she whispered, "I really, really do."

Hunter was lost. His mouth came down onto Brenna's before he realized he had moved. His hands slid over her buttocks and lifted her up to him, nestling her against his urgent arousal. She slid her tongue seductively into his mouth and he jerked in surprise, before succumbing to the desire rocketing through him.

"Brenna," he gasped, tearing his mouth from hers.

"Yes?" she said, eyebrows raised in innocence.

"Unless you want to put on a show for Cookie in the middle of the floor, you'd better cut that out."

"Cut what out?" she asked, rubbing her breasts against his chest.

"Oh, Lord." He moaned, rolling his eyes heavenward.

She traced the outline of his lips with the tip of her tongue. "Do you really have to go to the office?" she asked in a husky voice. Should she bat her eyelashes? she wondered. No, that was probably stretching it a bit. Heavens, this was fun. She was having an absolutely marvelous time turning

Hunter into putty. Not that she was in that great a shape herself. She wanted to drag him upstairs and plop him into bed. "Hmmm, Hunter?" she cooed. "Can't you stay a teeny-tiny bit longer?"

"You bet," he said, his voice raspy. "I mean, no!" He nearly jumped out of her arms. "I've got to get to work. I'll be here tonight at seven. Hell, make it six-thirty. Bye," he said, and strode out of the kitchen.

By six that evening, Brenna was more nervous than she cared to admit. She could hear Cindy chattering to Cookie in the living room, and knew Cindy was curious as to which of the new outfits Brenna would choose to dazzle Hunter the Hunk with.

The first layer was in place, and Brenna stared at herself in the mirror. The teddy was black. Black, silky, sexy, and lacy. It was cut low in the front, high on the sides, and was, she decided, disgraceful! Well, maybe not that bad. Alluring was a good word. So was ultrafeminine. Okay. On to the next layer.

The jumpsuit was also black, and hugged her figure in all the right places. She experimented with the front zipper. Down. Up a little. Down a tad more to expose just barely the tops of her breasts. Her hair was swept back from her face by shiny black combs, and she was taller by three inches due to black, strappy evening sandals. Mascara, blusher, lip gloss, then a generous spray of her new cologne, and she was ready!

"Well?" she said, standing in the doorway to the living room. "What do you think, Cindy?" Cindy's mouth dropped open and her eyes were wide as saucers. "Really?" Brenna said, smiling. "That good? Do you honestly think so?"

"Oh, my gosh," Cindy said, finding her voice. "You look . . . you look . . . I just can't believe how you look! I hope Hunter doesn't have a weak heart. Oh, Brenna, you're gorgeous! Sexy too! Cookie, take a gander at your mother. Isn't she a knock-out?" Cookie thumped his tail on the floor.

"I wish my butterflies would quit swooshing around," Brenna said, pressing her hand to her stomach. "I'm a nervous wreck. Oh, Lord, there's the buzzer."

"And here's my black shawl," Cindy said. "Go! I'll unlatch the door for the hunk."

"Bye," Brenna said weakly, then took a deep, steadying breath before leaving the room.

The soft glow of the single lamp in the down-stairs living room cast mysterious shadows over Hunter. As Brenna came down the stairs she could not clearly see his face. What she *could* see was his charcoal-gray suit, pale-blue shirt, and gray tie. Her heart quickened, as did her step, and she swal-lowed heavily as she approached him.

"Hello, Hunter," she said, stopping in front of him.

"You are," he said, his voice low and slightly strained, "the most beautiful woman I have ever seen. I've never seen you dressed so . . . so . . ."

"Sexy?" she asked, smiling at him.

"Yeah, sexy." He grinned. "The first guy that ogles you is going to have a broken jaw. You are really something."

"You look terrific, too, Hunter."

"Thank you. I think I forgot to kiss you hello."

"I think you did forget."

"However," he said, clearing his throat, "maybe I'd better pass for now. That outfit is wreaking havoc with my libido. It would be a lot safer if we just went on to dinner."

"Whatever you say, Hunter dear. Shall we go?" she said, ever so sweetly. Should she bat her eyelashes now? Oh, what the heck, why not?

"Is there something bothering your eyes?" he asked.

"No. Let's go."

Once in the car Hunter gave himself a firm lecture. Men who were nearly thirty years old, he told himself, did not make love to a woman in the front seat of a car.

But, merciful heaven, he was dying. Brenna was sensational in that black thing she was wearing. The zipper went all the way down the front. Lord. He had to get a grip on himself. But, dammit, he loved Brenna. Put that together with the way she looked and . . . No, the love factor was immaterial. He was here to be supportive until he was sure she had recovered from the MacPhee's blow, then he was walking out of her life. He was being a humanitarian of sorts.

Hunter had made reservations at the Cosmopolitan, a fabulous gourmet restaurant that offered a spectacular view of the city. Brenna felt like Cinderella. She was wearing snazzy new clothes, was dining in an elegant restaurant she'd never been to before, and Hunter was without a doubt the most handsome man in the room.

Cinderella? she mused. No, that wasn't who she wished to be. If she were, then her fantasy would all be over at midnight. She'd just stay who she was: Brenna MacPhee in love with Hunter Emerson.

As they ate, Brenna urged Hunter to tell her more about his childhood. He was the youngest in his family and, he admitted with a grin, had often teased his sisters unmercifully with rubber snakes in their beds, eavesdropping on their whispered conversations, and generally making a pest of himself. His favorite prank, he confided, was to wait in the bushes, then shine a flashlight on his sister and her date as they were about to kiss good night on the front porch.

"You were a rotten little kid," Brenna said, laughing in delight.

"On occasion," he agreed. "Innovative, though. I bought a bushel of grapes once to make wine. I stomped those buggers to death with my feet in the bathtub. All I got out of that was purple feet, and Annie standing over me with a stick until I scrubbed the tub to within an inch of its life."

"More coffee?" the waiter asked.

"Yes, please," Brenna said. The waiter poured the coffee, then walked away. "Hunter, why do you scowl every time that waiter comes to the table? Do you know him?"

"No. I just don't like the way he's looking at your zipper."

"My what?"

"Your zipper! He's seeing what I'm seeing, and I should be the only one seeing your— What I'm seeing."

"Oh," she said, peering down. "You mean the tops of my breasts?"

He moaned. "Brenna, please."

"Well, what he doesn't know is that there's not

much more to see than what he's seeing. I'm not exactly voluptuous, you know."

"You're perfect. You fill the palms of my hands like—" He stopped speaking and shifted in his chair as a shaft of heat shot through him. "Change the subject."

"Would you prefer that I pull the zipper up a bit? It goes up, and it goes down, and down, and down." She smiled brightly.

"Oh, Lord."

She grasped the zipper tab. "Well," she said, "your wish is my command. Up or down? Or is it north or south?"

"Are you ready to leave?" he asked through clenched teeth.

"Oh, well, sure, but what am I supposed to do about this zipper?"

"*I* will tend to the damn zipper!" he said, pushing himself to his feet.

"Okey-dokey," she said as she rose to join him.

In the car, Hunter continued to frown while Brenna smiled.

"You know, Hunter," she said pleasantly, "I've never seen where you live."

"It's just an average apartment."

"You can tell a lot about a person from the way they decorate, the books they own. You've seen my home. Shouldn't I see yours?"

"If you want to," he said, lifting a shoulder in a shrug. "I've got some good brandy. We'll have a nightcap."

"Lovely," she said, and wiggled in her seat. Then she wiggled again.

"Don't feel you have to answer this," Hunter

said, glancing over at her, "but do you have ants in your pants?"

"Oh, my, no. I just can't get over how marvelous my new silk teddy feels against my skin. It's so soft, like smooth, gentle hands stroking me all over. It's too bad you men have to wear cotton Jockeys. This teddy is fantastic. It sort of clings to me like—"

"That's it!" Hunter turned the corner onto a side street, pulled to the curb, and shut off the ignition. In the next instant, he hauled Brenna into his arms and spoke close to her lips. "You are driving me straight out of my mind," he said, then claimed her mouth with his.

Hello, Hunter Emerson! Brenna thought, circling his neck with her arms.

His tongue thrust deep into her mouth as his hand reached for the zipper on the jumpsuit. He inched it down, then slid his hand inside to cup her breast. The feel of silk covering her warm flesh was intoxicating. He flicked his thumb over her nipple, bringing it to a taut hardness. He leaned back against the door, taking Brenna with him, his mouth never leaving hers. One hand held her to him while the other roamed over the gentle slope of her buttocks. Her breasts were crushed against his chest and he wanted to see them, to touch them, kiss them. Groaning, he pressed his hips against hers, desperate for the release and ecstasy only Brenna could give him.

Suddenly he tore his mouth from hers. "I can't believe this," he said, his nose only a half inch from her. "I'm making out in a car. The windows are even fogged up. Fogged, for crying out loud!"

"Why are you yelling?" Brenna asked, trying to catch her breath.

"Because this is ridiculous," he said, lifting her back into her seat. "I'm not some horny kid out on a date. I'm a man!"

"There was never any doubt in my mind about *that,*" she said, smiling.

"And zip that zipper!"

"Yes, sir." She tried not to laugh as she did as instructed.

Hunter started the car and pulled away from the curb. His jaw was clenched, his knuckles white from his tight grip on the steering wheel.

"And furthermore," he went on, and Brenna jumped at his loud voice, "I'm taking you to *my* apartment, where we'll make love in *my* bed, because that's where you belong, Brenna MacPhee. With me! You are *my* woman."

"Goodness," she said, "you're certainly ferocious. Are you sure you're not part Scottish?"

He shot her a murderous glare, and she decided it was a good time to shut her mouth. She folded her hands primly in her lap and stared out the front window, a soft smile on her lips.

No, he wasn't Scottish, Hunter mentally stormed, he was crazy! A raving lunatic. He would have done it. He would have made love to Brenna on the front seat of his car. His well-ordered, logical, practical life had been shot straight to hell by Brenna MacPhee. It was a damn good thing he wasn't planning on hanging around her much longer, or he'd be certifiably insane.

When he left her, things would get back to normal, he reassured himself. He'd work twelve- and fourteen-hour days at his company, go home to his empty apartment, date the flash-and-dash gals once in a while. Fine. Great. That was exactly right. His attention would center on Hunter Emerson Consulting Corporation, where it belonged. He'd never see Brenna, the woman he loved, again. Excellent. Perfect. Everything would be on course, exactly as he'd planned it.

And the thought of all that brought on the blackest depression he had ever known.

Nine

Hunter's apartment was spacious and nicely furnished with dark wood furniture upholstered in warm earth tones.

"My mother fixed up the place," he said as he handed Brenna a snifter of brandy. "She said if I did it, I'd have nightmares forever."

"I like your mother very much," Brenna said, sitting down on the sofa. "It must be difficult for her."

"Decorating? No, she loves it. It's one of her hobbies." He sat down next to Brenna and sipped his brandy.

"No, I mean the animosity between you and your father. I'm sure she loves you both very much, and it must hurt her a great deal to see what's happened."

Hunter frowned. "She's not thrilled about it, but I wouldn't say she's hurt."

"She's the woman, the wife and mother, in the picture. She's caught in the middle. I think—"

"Brenna," he interrupted, "please don't think right now. Every time you do, *my* mind turns into scrambled eggs. So, don't think, just . . ." He took the snifter from her hand and set it on the coffee table. "Just feel."

"Are you about to take charge of my zipper?" she asked, smiling at him.

"You'd better believe it, lady."

And he did.

Much, much later, Brenna blessed the person who had invented zippers.

Brenna and Hunter lay quietly, their legs still entwined, their bodies sated from exquisite lovemaking. He slid his fingers through her hair, loving the feel of the silken strands, as she nestled her head on his shoulder.

"Brenna," he said.

"Hmm?" she murmured, trailing her fingers through the moist hair on his chest.

"I've gotten a handle on what it takes for you to run the Pet Palace. It's a great deal of hard labor that never seems to end. Have you ever considered doing something a little easier?"

"Well, the truth of the matter is that someday I'd like to breed show dogs. I've read tons of books, and I think I'd raise cocker spaniels. Then I'd sell them to people who'd enjoy training them and traveling to the different cities for shows. That part doesn't interest me. I'd rather stay home."

"Sounds good. Why don't you do it?"

"I can't right now. I need the income from the Pet Palace to pay my rent. Breeding show dogs requires special attention to the animals. I don't have time to do both."

"What if you had a silent partner?"

"A what?"

"Someone who invested money in your project, but left the decisions to you. Then you could close the Pet Palace to outside guests, and devote your energies to breeding the cockers."

"Great idea," she said, laughing softly. "I'll order a silent partner first thing tomorrow from the Sears catalogue."

"I'm serious, Brenna. I'd be willing to invest money as your silent partner."

"What?" she said, sitting up and looking at him. "That's ridiculous, Hunter. You need every penny you have for your own business."

"No I don't. I own all the equipment I need. I have to devote my time to my company, not my money. I'd feel a helluva lot better knowing you weren't working so hard."

"I see," she said quietly. "I'd get your money, Hunter Emerson Consulting Corporation would get your time and attention." Second place, her mind screamed. The money was like the MacPhee's unicorn. Second place!

"Hey," he said, gently rubbing her back, "you sound upset all of a sudden. I'm not trying to push you into anything. I'd really like to make an investment in your idea. Why don't you think about it for a while?"

"Yes. Yes, I will," she said, turning her head to hide the tears that had suddenly filled her eyes. "I appreciate your offer. It's very generous of you, Hunter. I really must get home." She slid off the bed, scooped her clothes up off the floor, and hurried into the bathroom.

Hunter frowned as the bathroom door closed. He'd definitely blown it, he thought, but he sure as hell didn't know how. He'd offered Brenna a chance to go on to her next dream. It wasn't charity, and she was intelligent enough to know that. They would draw up very official papers for their partnership, if that would make her happy. He'd honestly meant it when he'd said he didn't want her working so hard trying to run the Pet Palace. So what had he done to cause that stricken expression on her face? She'd looked like that when the MacPhee had given her the unicorn . . .

"Dammit!" he said, then swung off the bed and strode to the bathroom door. "Brenna, open up," he said, rapping on the door with his knuckles.

"Just a minute."

"Come on. I need to talk to you."

"Keep your pants on!"

"I haven't got any pants on! Open the door!"

She flung the door open and scowled at him. "What is your problem? Honestly, Hunter, are you planning on driving me home stark naked?"

He gripped her by the upper arms. "I am not the MacPhee!" he said fiercely.

"What?" Her eyes were wide with surprise at his outburst.

"That's what you're thinking, right? You see my offer of the money in the same light as the unicorns. You think it's conscience money, so I can go merrily on my way doing my thing with my business. Right, Brenna?"

"I—"

"Right?" he yelled, shaking her slightly.

"Yes!" Tears spilled onto her cheeks. "Yes, damn you, yes! Oh, I had such big plans," she said, a bitter edge to her voice. "I was going to come in first. First place in your life. I was so sure that you loved me, that you'd come to see that your goals for your company had been twisted out of focus by your father's attitude. I was going to work so hard to help you be a lobster, to shed your shell and grow, to need and love me as much as I do you."

"Brenna—"

"No! No more. I can't take any more. I don't want your money. I don't want to be fitted in around the edges of your life, to get the crumbs, just snatches of time with you. I won't be placed second for the rest of my days. I'm going to take care of myself, alone. I'll have Cookie, and like you said, he'll never make me cry. Take me home, Hunter. Take me home, and then—then get out of my life!"

"No! I love you, Brenna!"

"So you said once, in the throes of passion," she said, brushing past him.

"Dammit!" He grabbed her arm and his blue eyes were flashing with anger. "I'm telling you that I love you!"

"And I believe you," she said, looking directly at him. "But don't you see, Hunter? The MacPhee loves me too. I understand second-place love very well. I've decided that you're right. I deserve better than that from the man in my life. It's over between us. There's nothing left to say. I would appreciate it if you'd put some clothes on and drive me home. Or I could phone for a taxi if you prefer."

"I'd prefer to wring your neck!" he roared. "You're not dusting me off like this. How dare you insinuate that I'm not a lobster. That's a crummy thing to say, Brenna. And I'm not like the MacPhee. And I love you. And I've never said that to another woman before in my life. I know I love you because my drummer told me I do."

"And I," she said, her voice trembling, "have listened to my drummer too. I love you, Hunter, but I can't live the way you're asking me to."

"Brenna, please." He stared at the ceiling as he drew a shuddering breath. "Don't do this to us. Give us a chance. Give *me* a chance."

"I'll wait for you in the living room," she said, then turned and walked slowly out of the bedroom. She wouldn't cry, she told herself. Not here. Not now. She'd somehow wait until she got home, then she'd cry. For the next five years straight, she'd cry.

Hunter felt as though he'd been punched in the gut as he reached for jeans and a sweat shirt and pulled them on with shaking hands.

He was losing his Brenna! he thought with anguish. Dammit, no. This couldn't be happening. Yeah, okay, so he'd been going to leave her, but somewhere in the middle of the whole chaotic mess he'd changed his mind. When, he didn't know, but he'd definitely changed his mind. He loved Brenna MacPhee. Hell, he wanted to marry Brenna MacPhee. And instead he was losing her.

"No," he muttered, shoving his feet into loafers without bothering with socks. "No way." Easy, Emerson, he told himself. Slow down. Brenna was upset. Hell, *he* was upset. This was not the time to pursue this further. He'd take her home, then approach this thing reasonably, with logical analysis. He was a grown man. An intelligent, mature, grown man. And if things got any worse, he'd ask his mother for advice.

He walked into the living room, then halted abruptly, his throat tightening. Brenna was staring out the window, her back to him, head slightly bent, shoulders slumped. He wanted to gather her into his arms, hold her, declare his love over and over. He wanted to bellow in rage that he wasn't like the MacPhee, and plead with her in whispered urgency to give him the chance to prove it.

But he kept silent.

He *had* been like the MacPhee, he knew it, and the realization made him sick to his stomach. He could rationalize his actions until he was blue in the face, and the bottom line would remain the same. He had placed Brenna second in his life. Like a man possessed, he'd put Hunter Emerson Consulting Corporation first. And he'd done it in a desperate attempt to win his father's approval.

Hunter had buried it all so deeply within him, but now it was crystal clear. He'd worked so damn hard to prove his worth to his father, then had slowly comprehended that it was a losing battle. But the pattern for his life had been set by then—the grueling hours, the determination to succeed, his tunnel vision regarding his company. It was habit more than need, as he had little else to fill his life. Until Brenna. Until finding the only woman he had ever loved.

He would change it all now, put things in their proper perspective and balance. If Brenna would only give him another chance, he could prove to her that she would never again take second place in his world. But she knew, as he did, that he had taken so very much from her, and given so little in return.

"I'll drive you home now, Brenna," he said, his voice breaking slightly.

She turned to face him and their eyes met for a seemingly endless moment. A long, quiet, incredibly sad moment.

Then Brenna nodded and walked to the door. Hunter reached around her to open it, his body only inches from hers. He filled his senses with her sweet scent and his soul with love.

The drive to her home was made in total silence. Brenna stared out the side window and willed herself not to cry. Her heart hurt with an actual physical pain, and she was convinced that people really did die from a broken heart.

It was over, she thought. In a very few minutes she would say a final farewell to the only man she had ever loved. Oh, Hunter, she cried silently. She loved him with every breath in her body. But she couldn't stay with him. As she'd shed her shell she'd encompassed a world of more than just loving. She had found herself, her self-esteem and importance. For the first time in her life, she knew who Brenna MacPhee was.

She was a total woman, she realized. A person capable of being an equal partner in a relationship with a man. The first place she sought wasn't a pedestal, but the right to stand toe to toe, hand in hand, with the one she had chosen. He would not be married to his work or his wanderlust spirit, but to her. Second place was just too lonely. Just too incredibly lonely.

And so, she'd say good-bye to Hunter Emerson.

Hunter drove into the driveway, shut off the ignition, and stared straight ahead, his hands tightly gripping the steering wheel. He drew a deep breath, then turned to look at her.

"Brenna," he said in a low voice, "I—I'll see you in."

"No, please don't," she said as she opened the door. "Please don't make this any harder than it is."

"I love you, Brenna."

"And I love you," she said, a sob catching in her throat. "I guess our drummers got a little confused when they sent the messages. We weren't meant to be together. Good-bye, Hunter." She slipped out of the car and ran to the house.

"Ah, Brenna," Hunter said, smacking his palm against the steering wheel. "The drummers didn't screw it up, *I* did." He waited until she was safely inside the house, then started the car again. "I'm going to get you back, Brenna," he said to the night. "Somehow. I'm not the MacPhee and, dammit, I *am* a lobster."

With his jaw set in a tight line, he drove away, looking back once with an ache in his heart at the Pet Palace.

Brenna walked slowly up the stairs, hesitated outside her living-room door, then entered.

"Hi," Cindy said. "You're alone? Oh. Well, tell all. What did Hunter the Hunk think of the femme fatale, the sexiest outfit of the decade?"

Brenna burst into tears.

"Oh, good grief," Cindy said, jumping to her feet. "Oh, dear. Oh, my. Brenna?" Cookie wiggled and wagged his tail. "Brenna, what happened? Do we hate Hunter now?"

"I love him!" Brenna wailed.

"Because he makes you so happy, right? What is going on here?"

Brenna sank onto the sofa and wept her way through her tale of woe, halting only long enough for Cindy to dash into the bathroom to bring her a handful of tissues.

". . . and so it's over," Brenna finished, still sniffling. "Done. Finished. Kaput. And my heart hurts. It's splintering into a million pieces."

"Do hearts do that?" Cindy asked. "Never mind. Oh, Brenna, what can I say that will help? I'm so sorry this happened. I swear, they're just not making drummers like they used to. You deserve more than Hunter Emerson was willing to give you."

"I love him!" Brenna said, and the tears started again.

"Really? Gosh, you could have fooled me." She threw up her hands. "What a mess. Cookie, quit smiling. Can't you see we're having a crisis here?" Cookie flopped down onto the floor in a dejected heap. "That's better. Brenna, would you like me to spend the night so you don't have to be alone?"

"No, you go on home," Brenna said, then blew her nose. "Thank you for listening, Cindy. I'll be fine, really I will." In ten or twenty years, she added silently. Maybe.

"Will you go right to bed? You're exhausted."

"Yes. Yes, I will."

"I really am sorry," Cindy said, giving Brenna a quick hug. "I sure did like Hunter the Hunk."

"And I love him!"

Cindy rolled her eyes as she left the room. "I know, I know," she said. "I'll call you soon and see how you're holding up. Bye."

"Bye," Brenna said. She shut off the light and

shuffled into the bedroom. "Come on, Cookie," she said. "It's late. You're due to start snoring."

Once in bed, Brenna pulled the blankets up to her chin, stared up into the darkness, and then, for the lack of anything better to do, she cried. She loved Hunter. She missed Hunter. She wanted and needed Hunter, and he was gone. So she cried.

At one o'clock the next afternoon, Maggie marched into Hunter's office, planted her hands flat on his desk, leaned forward, and glared at him.

"Hunter Emerson," she said, "I will grant you one last request before I murder you!"

"Huh?" he said, looking at her in surprise.

"You've snapped my head off ever since you stormed in here this morning, you don't answer the phone when I buzz you, the list is endless. In short, Mr. Emerson, what in the hell is the matter with you?"

"It—I—Brenna," he said miserably. "I've lost my Brenna."

"What did you do to perfect Brenna, you dum-dum?" Maggie asked, planting her hands on her hips.

"Well, you see, it's like this . . ."

When Hunter finished his story, he looked at Maggie with a hopeful expression on his face.

"Any brilliant ideas?" he asked.

"Tar and feathers come to the front of my mind."

"Maggie!"

"Okay, I'm sorry. I'd love to say I told you so, but I'll hold myself back. Hunter, you blew it, pure and simple. Somehow you have got to prove to Brenna that you have things in their proper perspective now, that you realize this company is important, but that it no longer consumes your life."

"I know that, but saying it to her won't do any good. The MacPhee makes promises all the time, but never keeps them. Brenna wouldn't believe that I've changed."

"You must make her see that you want to be a part of her world, Hunter. You placed her second, and that was wrong. Did you ever buy her an ice cream cone? I remember you told me she likes ice cream cones."

"No, I never bought her an ice cream cone," he said, raking his fingers through his hair.

"The phone is ringing. We'll talk again, if you want to. Think about it, Hunter. Think about ice cream cones, and whatever else is important to Brenna. And for Pete's sake, don't be logical!"

"Thanks, Maggie," he said absently, already staring off into space.

At four o'clock, a weary, red-eyed Brenna answered the door at the Pet Palace.

"Brenna MacPhee?" The man on the front porch asked.

"Yes?"

"Delivery, ma'am," he said. He opened a cooler at his feet and gingerly retrieved his cargo.

Brenna gasped. "An ice cream cone? A triple-decker ice cream cone?"

"Yes, ma'am," the man said, beaming. "You have here Marshmallow Marvel, Bubble Gum Delight, and Raspberry Rhapsody. Oh, please note the cherry on the top. This is Happy Harvey's Ice Cream Haven ice cream. The best in Portland,

Oregon. Compliments of—" he pulled a card from his pocket—"a Mr. Hunter Emerson."

"Hunter? Hunter sent me an ice cream cone? That's crazy. He's never had time to—" A smile lit up her face. "That's the most beautiful ice cream cone I've ever seen."

"Classy, huh? Well, here you go." He handed it to her. "Have a nice day."

"Yes, thank you," she said, her gaze fixed on her treat as she closed the door. "Oh, Hunter," she whispered, "what are you trying to tell me?" Should she call him and thank him? she wondered. No, she'd never be able to hear his voice without falling apart. She'd have to think this through, try to figure out what it meant. In the meantime? "I'm going to eat my ice cream!"

"One triple-decker ice cream cone delivered to Miss Brenna MacPhee," Hunter said to Maggie.

"Check. You're doing great. What's next?"

"Do you suppose there's someplace in this town where a guy can buy a rainbow?"

The rainbow arrived at the Pet Palace the next morning at ten. It was huge, made of flowers, and Brenna had the distinct impression that it was meant to go around a horse's neck at the finish of a race. It was absolutely beautiful. She smiled through the remainder of the day, but still could not muster the courage to call Hunter.

When Cindy popped in on Saturday morning to babysit while Brenna went shopping, Brenna brought her up-to-date on what had taken place.

"Oh, wow!" Cindy said. "This is unreal. What else did you tell Hunter you were crazy about?"

"I don't remember. I really don't."

"The suspense is killing me."

"Oh, Cindy, I'm trying not to read too much into all this, but I can't help myself. I think Hunter's trying to tell me that the things that are important to me, are important to him too. Do you realize what that could mean? I'd be in first place. Oh, I don't know. I'm so frightened. I mustn't forget the emphasis he places on his company."

"Take it slow and easy, Brenna. The ball is in Hunter the Hunk's court. So far, he's doing super!"

On Sunday morning, Charlotte Emerson found her son crawling around the backyard of the Emerson home on his hands and knees.

"Good morning, dear," she said calmly.

" 'Lo," he mumbled, not looking up.

"Should I ask what you're doing, or am I better off not knowing?"

"I'm looking for four-leaf clovers."

"Of course, how silly of me. I should have known."

"They're for Brenna, Mother. She makes wishes on four-leaf clovers."

"Well, in that case," Charlotte said, dropping to her knees beside him, "let's find her a basketful."

"I love her, Mom," Hunter said quietly, looking at his mother. "I love her, I've lost her, and I want her back."

"Bless you, dear," Charlotte said, quick tears filling her eyes. "Now! Get busy. We have four-leaf clovers to find."

"Mother, I'm very sorry if my problems with Dad have hurt you. Do you think he'd like to go golfing with me sometime?"

"Yes, I think he would. Thank you, Hunter. More than I can say. Oh, look. I found a four-leaf clover!"

Tears were streaming down Brenna's face when she opened the door to Cindy on Monday morning. Brenna was clutching a wicker basket filled with four-leaf clovers.

"I cut class," Cindy said, bouncing in the door. "I couldn't wait to see what the hunk had done next. Oh-h-h, four-leaf clovers! Are we happy?"

"Thrilled," Brenna said, sniffling. "Hunter is the dearest, sweetest, most wonderful man in the world. I love him so much."

"Have you called him to thank him for all this?"

"No, not yet. I'm still so afraid to believe he really means it. Hunter Emerson Consulting Corporation is there, it's real, and I can't ignore the place it has in Hunter's life. He— Cindy, where's Cookie? He was right here when you came in. Did you lock the door behind you? Oh, no! Cookie!"

"Do I look all right?" Hunter asked, stopping by Maggie's desk and straightening his tie.

"Gorgeous. I'm surprised you've come down off your Brenna cloud long enough to prepare for this presentation."

"This is the biggest job I've ever gone after for this company, Maggie. I want it, I really do."

"You'll get it, Hunter," she said, smiling warmly. "You're a top-notch cost analyst. You're also a very nice man. Excuse," she said, as the telephone rang. "Hunter Emerson Consulting Corporation. . . . Pardon me? . . . I'm sorry, but I can't understand you. Could you slow down a little?"

"Who is it?" Hunter asked.

"What?" Maggie said. "Hunter? Yes, he's here, but . . . We don't sell cookies, we—"

"Cookie?" Hunter said. "Give me that." He snatched the receiver from a startled Maggie. "Hello? This is Hunter Emerson."

"Oh, Hunter, thank God," Cindy said, sobbing. "It's Cookie. . . . And Brenna went, but she was so upset I didn't think she should drive. . . . It's all my fault. . . . I promised to stay here to babysit—"

"Cindy," Hunter yelled, "what happened? Why is Brenna upset? What about Cookie?"

"The door . . . He got out. . . . Oh, Hunter, Cookie was hit by a car!"

"No! Where's Brenna?"

"She took Cookie to the vet. She was crying and . . . Oh, Hunter, I left the door unlocked and—"

"Cindy, what vet?"

"Um, let's see. Dr. Culbertson on Third Street."

"I'm on my way."

"Oh, thank you, thank you. I'm so sorry."

"Take it easy, Cindy. I'm leaving for the vet's right now," Hunter said, and hung up.

"Hunter?" Maggie said. "What in the world is—"

"I've got to get over there," he said, flipping through the phone book. "Culbertson on Third. Where on Third?"

"You have that presentation to give. Hunter, you'll lose the chance at getting that job."

"Call them. See if they'll postpone. I've got to go."

"Go where?"

"To Brenna, Maggie. To my Brenna. She needs me, and nothing else matters."

"Then hurry," she said, smiling at him. "You've got your priorities exactly right, and I love you!"

Brenna paced back and forth in the reception room of the veterinarian's office, wringing her hands as unnoticed tears poured down her cheeks. Please, don't die, Cookie, she pleaded silently. Oh, please, please, don't die.

The time passed slowly as she continued to pace, staring often at the door that led to the room where Cookie had been taken. He'd been so still, so frighteningly still, his heartbeat barely discernible.

"Don't leave me, Cookie," she whispered. "I love you so much."

Suddenly the outer door of the office burst open and Brenna jumped in surprise at the loud noise.

"Hunter!" she gasped.

He hurried to her and pulled her into his arms.

"I got here as quickly as I could," he said. "How's Cookie? How's our Cookie, Brenna?"

"I don't know," she said as she wrapped her arms around his waist. "He's unconscious. How did you know?"

"Cindy called me, and I came right over. You're white as a ghost. Come sit on this couch."

He pulled her down next to him on the couch, holding her tightly. She leaned her head on his shoulder and sighed, a long, wobbling sigh.

"Hang in there, babe," he said. "I'm right here with you. You're not alone, Brenna, not anymore, not ever again."

"The presents. The ice cream cone, and the rainbow, and . . ."

"We'll cover it all later. We need to talk, really talk. I—"

"Brenna?" a man said, coming out of the back room.

"Oh, Dr. Culbertson," Brenna said. She rushed across the room to the doctor, with Hunter close behind. "How is he? How is Cookie?"

The doctor chuckled. "He has one economy-size headache. Cookie suffered a mild concussion. You'll have to keep him quiet for a few days and watch for potential danger signs, but I'd say he's going to be fine."

"Oh, thank God," Brenna whispered.

"Takes more than a bump on the head to keep our boy down," Hunter said smugly. "Can we take him home now?"

"Sure," the doctor said. "I'll give you a list of instructions. I don't want that yo-yo staying here. I'd have to keep all my doors locked!"

Cookie wagged his tail when Brenna and Hunter entered the back room, then rolled over and stuck his paws in the air.

"Don't ham it up," Hunter said. "You're going to get enough sympathy as it is." He gently lifted Cookie into his arms. "We're going home, buddy."

"Hunter, you're getting white fur all over that gorgeous suit," Brenna said.

"Doesn't matter. I'll put Cookie in your car. May I follow you home, Brenna?"

"Yes," she said softly. "Yes, please do."

Bedlam reigned at the Pet Palace when the patient arrived. Cindy laughed and cried, hugged everyone on two feet and four, then left with the announcement that she was taking to her bed for a week. Clancey howled, then shut up when he realized no one was paying any attention to him. Cookie basked in his glory, tail thumping, tongue hanging out of his mouth, until he finally fell asleep in his favorite spot on the floor by Brenna's bed. And he snored.

Silence fell over the living room as Brenna and Hunter stood looking at each other across the length of the room.

"I'm really glad he's okay," Hunter finally said.

"Thank you for coming like you did, Hunter. It meant so much to me to have you there."

"That's where I want to be, with you, always. Oh, Brenna, I've missed you so much, and I love you so much. I sent the ice cream cone, and all that other stuff, to try and convince you how desperately I want to be a part of your wonderful world. I need you in my life. Lord, how I need you."

"I—I want to believe you, Hunter, but I'm so frightened. The gifts were precious and I'll treasure them, but there's still your company. I know it comes first, will always come first with you."

He walked to the telephone sitting on the end table and dialed a number. "Maggie?" he said, a few moments later. "Yeah, everything is fine. So? What's the verdict? . . . Oh? They said since I didn't show the deal was off?"

"What?" Brenna whispered.

"I see," he went on. "Hunter Emerson Consulting Corporation took it in the chops because I was with Brenna?"

"Oh, no," Brenna said.

"Well, Maggie, my message to those hot dogs is:

Stuff it!" he said, then replaced the receiver with a thud.

"Oh, Hunter, what have you done?" Brenna asked.

"I have," he said, walking slowly toward her, "fallen in love for the first time in my life. I have listened to my drummer and filled my heart with his song. I've straightened out my priorities at long last, and brought a human quality into my life of logic and overorganizing. Thanks to you, I've faced the truth about my compulsion to prove things to my father, then later to myself. I have, I hope, earned the title of lobster. You are my life, Brenna MacPhee. I'm asking you to marry me, have my babies, share, laugh, and love with me. I'm offering you all I have, my heart, mind, body, and soul. And first place, next to me, forever."

"Hunter . . ."

He stopped several feet away from her and held out his hand. "Please, Brenna?" he said, his voice choked with emotion. "Please?"

She flung herself into his arms and was lifted off her feet as he held her tightly to his chest.

"Yes! Oh, yes," she said, fresh tears shimmering in her eyes. "I'll marry you, Hunter. I love you so much, so very, very much."

He slid her down his body until her feet touched the floor and gazed at her, making no attempt to hide the tears in his own eyes. Then he lowered his head and claimed her mouth in a soft kiss that soon grew urgent as they clung to each other.

"I want to make love to you," he murmured.

"Yes. I want you too."

"We have so many plans to discuss, like a

wedding, getting you started raising those cocker spaniels, and—"

"Later," she said. "Later."

"Oh, Brenna, I came so close to losing you forever."

"We're together now, Hunter. That's all that matters."

"You do realize what I'm sacrificing, don't you?"

"What do you mean?"

"Brenna, I will never, ever again be able to eat lobster! Those brave little buggers taught me so much that I feel as though every one of them is a personal friend of mine."

"We'll make up for it," she said, laughing, "with a lifetime of ice cream cones!"

They made sweet, slow, exquisite love that spoke of trust, commitment, forgiveness, and greater understanding. Later they slept, lying close, their heads resting on the same pillow. Once Brenna stirred and opened her eyes. Then she smiled as she drifted back to sleep, carrying with her the memory of the sound that had awakened her.

The gentle rat-a-tat-tat of a drummer.

THE EDITOR'S CORNER

Home for the Holidays! Certainly home is the nicest place to be in this upcoming season . . . and coming home, finding a home, perfecting one are key elements in each of our LOVESWEPTs next month.

First, in Peggy Webb's delightful **SCAMP OF SALTILLO,** LOVESWEPT #170, the heroine is setting up a new home in a small Mississippi town. Kate Midland is a witty, lovely, committed woman whose determination to save a magnolia tree imperiled by a construction crew brings her into face-to-face confrontation with Saltillo's mayor, Ben Adams. What a confrontation! What a mayor! Ben is self-confident, sensual, funny, generous . . . and perfect for Kate. But it takes a wacky mayoral race—including goats, bicycles, and kisses behind the bandstand—to bring these two fabulous people together. A romance with real heart and humor!

It is their homes—adjacent apartments—that bring together the heroine and hero in **FINNEGAN'S HIDEAWAY,** LOVESWEPT #171, by talented Sara Orwig. Lucy Reardon isn't really accident prone, but try to convince Finn Mundy of that. From the moment he spots the delectable-looking Lucy, her long, long shapely legs in black net stockings, he is falling . . . for her, with her, even

(continued)

off a ladder on top of her! But what are a few bruises, a minor broken arm compared to the enchantment and understanding Lucy offers? When Finn's brothers—and even his mother—show up on the doorstep, the scene is set for some even wilder misunderstandings and mishaps as Finn valiantly tries to handle that mob, his growing love for Lucy, law school exams, and his failing men's clothing business. A real charmer of a love story!

In the vivid, richly emotional **INHERITED,** LOVESWEPT #172, by gifted Marianne Shock, home is the source of a great deal of the conflict between heroine Tricia Riley and hero Chase Colby. Tricia's father hires Texas cowboy Chase to run Tricia's Virginia cattle ranch. Their attraction is instantaneous, explosive . . . as powerful as their apprehensions about sharing the running of the ranch. He brings her the gift of physical affection, for she was a child who lost her mother early in life and had never known her father's embrace or sweet words. She gives Chase the gift of emotional freedom and, at last, he can confide feelings he's never shared. But before these two ardent, needy people can come together both must deal with their troublesome pasts. A love story you'll cherish!

In **EMERALD FIRE,** LOVESWEPT #173, that marvelous storyteller Nancy Holder gives us a delightful couple in Stacy Livingston and Keith

(continued)

Mactavish . . . a man and a woman who seem worlds apart but couldn't be more alike at heart. And how does "home" play a part here? For both Stacy and Keith home means roots—his are in the exotic land of Hawaii, where ancestors and ancient gods are part of everyday life. Stacy has never felt she had any real roots, and has tried to find them in her work toward a degree as a marine biologist. Keith opens his arms and his home to her, sharing his large and loving family, his perceptions of sensual beauty and the real romance of life. You'll relish this exciting and provocative romance!

Home for the Holidays . . . in every heartwarming LOVESWEPT romance next month. Enjoy. And have a wonderful Thanksgiving celebration in your home!

Warm wishes,

Carolyn Nichols

Carolyn Nichols
Editor
LOVESWEPT
Bantam Books, Inc.
666 Fifth Avenue
New York, NY 10103